ACCIDENT BY DESIGN

Walter Fletcher lives at the end of one of the remote valleys in the Forest of Dean. An old man, but still vigorous, he is determined to assert his independence when his family try to persuade him to move out of the big house he has lived in for forty years.

But it is a fatal decision, for within two days he is dead. His death is at first presumed to be accidental, and it is his granddaughter, home for the funeral, who raises doubts about it. Super-intendent Lambert and Sergeant Hook find to their embarrassment that the girl's suspicions of foul play are only too well founded.

The instinct of the small community of people in this secluded part of the Forest is to protect their own, and, as they close ranks, the police investigation becomes increasingly difficult . . . especially when it emerges that this killing is prob-ably the work of either the family or a close friend of the victim.

As Lambert and Hook probe the temperaments of those who were closest to the dead man, J. M. Gregson reveals his customary sure grasp of dialogue and motive. Somewhere among these likeable, even admirable, men and women, a murderer is watching events unfold. The pace of the investigation is swift, and the solution both unexpected and intriguing.

ACCIDENT
BY DESIGN

J. M. Gregson

HarperCollins*Publishers*

Collins Crime
An imprint of HarperCollins*Publishers*
77–85 Fulham Palace Road, London W6 8JB

First published in Great Britain
in 1996 by Collins Crime

1 3 5 7 9 10 8 6 4 2

© J. M. Gregson 1996

The Author asserts the moral right to be
identified as the author of this work

A catalogue record for this book is
available from the British Library

ISBN 0 00 232578 0

Set in Meridien and Bodoni

Photoset by Rowland Phototypesetting Ltd
Bury St Edmunds, Suffolk
Printed and bound in Great Britain by
HarperCollinsManufacturing Glasgow

1

No one knew afterwards what had provoked the row.

At one moment, they were balancing plates and saucers awkwardly upon their knees in the crowded little lounge. At the next, voices which had been subdued, even faltering, were raised in sudden anger.

'I know how I feel. That's what matters. And that's all there is to it.' The old man's voice rose on each querulous assertion.

'But why on earth can't you listen to reason for once, without flying off the handle?' Alan's tone marked the end of patience, the moment when frustration dipped into anger. Father and son stood facing each other in the bay window, not seeing the neat garden outside and its sunlit, irrelevant flowers. Two large, heavy men, with the family resemblance unmistakable, breathing heavily, conscious that this was ridiculous, but unable to prise themselves out of it. They were the only two people without chairs in the room, standing toe to toe in ill-matched confrontation.

A family row, with the desultory conversation around it stilled into sudden silence by the strength of domestic passions. Both participants unable to stand back, to take a detached view of the issues involved, as they might have in other, less personal circumstances.

There came then a female voice from below them, pleading nervously, until it rose into what was almost a whine. 'All we're asking you to do, Dad, is to consider the idea. That's all that Alan's saying. That's reasonable, isn't it? There's no compulsion.'

The intervention pleased neither of the men, for they had moved beyond compromise. The whine irritated them. The younger man rounded upon his wide-eyed, anxious sister. 'It's no good, Alison. You should know enough about him by now to realize that we're wasting our time. This whole business has been just that: a waste of time for all of us.'

Amidst the sudden silence and the pressure of the upturned faces, Alan looked round for an escape. He wanted to turn his back on his white-haired, stubborn father, to storm out of the room, out of this familiar house. He needed the release of physical movement for his resentment against this obdurate old man. And he was vaguely aware that he might show himself in a worse light, might be drawn into reckless overstatements, if he was left to pursue this fruitless mission any longer.

Words were not Alan Fletcher's strength; now that he lived mostly alone, he sometimes went for days without using them. His father would browbeat him into defeat if he kept up the struggle; it had happened since he was a boy. He wanted to finish the scene, to get away from this too-public argument, whilst he still felt there was right on his side. But there was no clear path out of the crowded room. The white, expectant faces ranged across it like a barricade.

Instead, it was his father who left. Walter Fletcher too looked at the faces, realizing for the first time the reason why they had come into his house today, deciding that the family gathering he had thought so innocent and spontaneous had been carefully organized to drive him into a corner.

'I've had enough of this!' the old man said. And then he whirled away from his son, stumbling awkwardly between the armchairs and the crockery, passing close to familiar faces that belonged now to strangers and busy lips that were suddenly stilled with embarrassment.

It seemed to take him a long time to reach the cool relief of the outdoors and the low, late-summer sun. He chose the side garden, beneath the high weather-boarded gable, with its long narrow lawn and the border of perennials beside it. He would be safe here from the eyes which would study him through the big bay window of the room he had just left if he had gone to the front lawn.

'Interfering buggers!' Walter muttered softly to himself. He never swore in public, never had done, even when he had worked alongside men who scarcely noticed their expletives. Yet he found himself swearing more and more in private nowadays. He had only begun to do it quite recently, he thought. He could not remember doing it in the first years after Dorothy had died.

Sometimes, these days, the whole world seemed to be against him. And it was no help being rich, richer than he had ever thought to be in his youth. That only seemed to make things more complicated.

Yet he knew those people in the house cared about him, were generally anxious about his welfare. Most of them, anyway: he found that he was less sure of his ground about these things as time went on. Perhaps that was because he had no one to confide in.

Suddenly, as the gathering starlings swooped over his head and rose high against the darkening blue sky, he wished his granddaughter had been here this afternoon. He found it easier to talk to Hannah than anyone, these days. He didn't even mind letting her see that he was lonely and a little afraid. Perhaps it was easier because years ago she had confided all her childhood fears to him. He smiled, remembering that long-gone day when he had persuaded ten-year-old Hannah on this very spot that the big school might not be so bad after all.

A moment later, he found his hand suddenly full of poppy seed-heads; he must have removed them unconsciously as he moved along the border. He sighed, watching one of them explode quietly into his palm, spilling the seeds carefully on to the lawn, where they could do no damage as they tried to spring into life. 'I'm not that old!'

7

he murmured. At that moment, it seemed important to convince himself of the fact.

'You all right, Dad?' The slim figure of Alison, Hannah's mother, was beside him. Why should he think of her like that, he wondered, instead of as his own daughter? It was she who had tried to still the conflict in the house. Her nervousness had turned her normally soft and attractive voice into that unattractive whimper. He felt suddenly sorry for her, that she should have been driven to that.

'Yes. I'm all right. I just wish people would get on with their own lives and leave me to get on with mine.' Walter wished he could touch her, hold her as he had when she was a child, emphasizing that he loved her, whatever their differences, that love made arguments unimportant.

But he could not do it. He had scarcely touched her for years now, apart from formal meetings and goodbyes; to clasp her to him here would seem awkward, even unnatural, for both of them. He should make the effort, he knew, should throw his arms round her and defeat that stupid, creeping awkwardness. But he could not find the energy to do it.

He could not know that Alison was willing him to hug her, even as she knew he would not, wanting to stretch both hands out to him in that old gesture which she had not used since her mother's funeral nine years ago.

Instead, she said dully, repeating the arguments which had already failed, 'This place is too big for you now, Dad. We have to look to the future, you know.' She turned her bright, dark eyes hopefully up to him, hoping to convince him of her love, even when she knew the words would fail. But he had turned away from her.

He didn't like that 'We'. It was the way the health visitor spoke to him when she visited. And it seemed to include Alison's husband, the schoolteacher, the only man inside the house who wasn't a Forester. Walter looked automatically at the wooded valley that ran away below the house to the village, then at May Hill to the north, the rise that marked the limits of the Forest of Dean. He put a surly emphasis on the pronouns as he said, '*I'll* think of the future when it suits *me*. I'm happy here, for the present.'

'But you're not getting any younger, Dad. We all worry about you being up here on your own. Jim says if anything went wrong – '

'Jim says far too much. He wants to keep his opinions for that school of his. Country's full of young hooligans now. Time they did something about it.' The old man's lips closed sullenly, like a child's as it sets its face against the logic it does not want to hear.

And Alison, looking up at the handsome elevations of the house where she had been born and known much happiness, found she could say no more. There was reason in what her father said, and they were here because they had their own needs for him to move out of his house. She was suddenly disgusted by the shabbiness of their schemes and the clumsiness of the manoeuvre which had brought them to High Beeches today.

Father and daughter went back indoors a few minutes later, and the rest of the family put a brave face on the situation. Alan and Chris Fletcher were washing up. The two sons, so physically dissimilar, were making the most of the routine jokes about role reversal. Alan was washing: his broad hands placed the crockery with excessive care on the rack outside the sink, as if he feared that it might at any moment escape his unpractised grasp. Chris was drying, standing a little awkwardly upon his one sound leg, in that stance which Alison always found so touching, his slender fingers drying cutlery as if it was something much more precious.

Her husband, Jim, was as usual a little to one side, supposedly putting away the plates and cups, but not quite certain where each item should go. As usual, he gave the impression of a bit-player on the edge of the scene, with no very useful part to play in the main action. He was talking to Chris about books; the conversation made good sense because both of them were enthusiasts. Yet it carried an air of artificiality. Both of them knew that this was

9

no more than a diversion from the main business of the afternoon, which had failed.

Alison felt a sudden, illogical fury with her husband, that he should have been so ineffective, should have taken so little part in this, when he was as anxious as any of them that her father should leave the old house. Why couldn't Jim force things into happening, take his destiny into his own hands, as other men seemed able to do?

There was not much else to be done, now. They all, even Walter, tried to ensure that the gathering broke up without further high words. There were bright snippets of conversation, compliments to Alison on the baking she had brought here with her, praise for Walter on the condition of his garden after the long dry summer.

Everyone tried very hard to pretend that nothing had happened.

2

Walter Fletcher was still annoyed next morning. He found himself wanting to do something to pique the family. He knew that was childish. But they were trying to treat him like a child, weren't they?

He decided he would go to see Brenda Collins.

Brenda was a widow, five years younger than him, buxom even in her late sixties, with grey-white hair always neatly trimmed into a becoming frame for her round and cheerful face. She lived scarcely more than half a mile from him, on the fringe of the small village of Endean which was the human gathering point of this quiet valley.

She was at the gate as he arrived, almost as if she had been expecting him. The bright morning had a tinge of autumn sharpness and Brenda's face shone with health. Her brown, humorous eyes assessed her friend as he came up the lane with his steady, rolling gait, his shoulders rounded into the stoop which was becoming more noticeable as the years passed.

As always, they were at ease with each other immediately. She did not ask him why he had come, and he felt no need to tell her. Both of them knew that if there was a reason, it would emerge easily enough in due course. Walter lingered a while with her in the garden, savouring the autumn tints of her small collection of maples as the low October sun fell full upon them.

They waved to Grace Jackson as she returned down the lane from her milk delivery. Walter even asked Grace about her children. He was quite anxious that his presence at Brenda's cottage should be noted: it was his riposte to those who had planned to transfer him from his own house to what he thought of as a nursing home.

They went into the mellow stone cottage to the reassuring scent of coffee – almost, he thought again, as if Brenda had been expecting him. He sat contentedly in his usual armchair, by the fireplace with its logs set ready to light. It was the chair, he surmised, where Brenda's husband, a taciturn farmer who had died in the same year as his own wife, had been used to sit in the evenings.

He knew that his family speculated about the possibility of his marrying again. That was why he wanted them to know that he had come here today. Brenda Collins was their only candidate for the role of a second, unwelcome, Mrs Fletcher. He had done work at her house for her, increasingly over the last three years.

And Walter Fletcher and Brenda Collins were comfortable with each other, in a manner they would certainly not have been thirty years earlier. They had even discussed the possibility of marriage, openly and without embarrassment. Which meant that it was most unlikely to happen. But there was no need to tell other people that.

At first they talked safe talk, about the mystery of how another summer could have gone so quickly, about the pleasures of autumn as the oaks and the beeches began to illuminate the Forest with their autumn glories. Brenda said, 'I might go to see my Alice in New Zealand. In February, I think; miss a month of our winter.'

'You say that every year. This time you should go. You can afford it.' He grinned at her, aware that he was talking to her as bluntly as any relative.

'Perhaps I shall. Yes, you're right. I'll go into Cinderford tomorrow and ask about flights.'

'Get it fixed up. I can run you to the airport, if they fly from Bristol.' But he knew she had her own son in Gloucester, who would see to such things if the need arose. He felt a little surge of illogical resentment against children in general. Perhaps it was really an anger against the dependence he feared, which he saw creeping ever nearer with the passing years.

'Had the family round yesterday,' he said. She said nothing, sensing that this was an introduction to something more serious. Her silence made him feel foolishly dramatic as he said, 'They want to put me into a home.'

She looked at him, lips wrinkling into a smile, concern behind the twinkle in her eyes. 'Not put you in, I'm sure, Walter. No one moves *you* around like furniture.'

He was grateful to her for that, even though it diminished a little the impact of what he wanted to say. 'Well, they said it wasn't a home really. "Sheltered accommodation", they said, whatever that is. I think you have your own place, but there's a warden to keep an eye on you.' He stopped abruptly: this didn't sound as bad as he had intended it to.

And Brenda echoed his thought. 'It doesn't sound too bad, Walter. Preserve your independence, but have someone around to keep an eye on you. We might be glad of that eventually, as we get older.'

Her tone did not sound convinced, and he grinned at her. 'Thinking of doing it yourself, are you, Bren?'

He didn't often shorten her name like that. It took her back to her childhood, when she had been a small girl trailing behind her brother, dragging her toes in the dust of those prewar summers which seemed now to have been so long. Walter had appeared to her child's eyes immensely older and stronger than her.

She smiled at him from the other side of the fireplace, then glanced round the comfortable room, with its heavy furniture, its polished brasses gleaming softly on the polished wood. 'I shan't be going from here until I have to. No more than you will, Walter!'

They giggled a little together, conspirators against the young and their foolish ideas. Then, lest she appear too critical of his children, she added, 'But I'm sure they meant well,

13

Walter. They care about you, you know, Alison and your lads.'

'Maybe so. But I'll go when I'm ready, not when they think I should. And I'm not ready yet awhile.' He allowed his Gloucestershire accent to come out strongly on the thought, as if it were in itself a rebuttal of their plans.

Then he grinned, a secret, schoolboy grin, which was not lost upon his conspirator across the hearth. 'What be you planning, Walter?' she said, the accent she had once striven to lose suddenly as strong as his.

He looked at her sharply. He had not thought he was as transparent as that. Then he relaxed, happy to share the thought which had only that moment hardened into a decision. 'I'm going to paint the outside o' my place,' he said, settling back comfortably into the armchair, as if he could only savour the prospect satisfactorily in complete comfort.

'What, the outside woodwork?'

'Woodwork, gutters, the lot. I'll start by creosoting the two gable ends. They're ready for it, after the good summer we've had.'

She was silent, picturing the high, weather-boarded gables beneath the soaring eaves of the big house on the hill. She was suddenly anxious for her friend. 'There's a lot of that house of yours, Walter.' She was careful not to add 'and you're getting a bit old for that sort of work'.

He said, 'I can take my time. Make a good job of it, that way. There's no need to rush at it.'

'I don't like to think of you perched up a ladder all that time.' This time she almost added, 'You're not as steady as you used to be', but she stopped herself just in time, as she saw his mouth setting into that determined line. Men were such stubborn creatures sometimes, and this one more often than most.

'I've been up ladders often enough. They don't scare me.'

Now she found a way of saying it. 'You're not getting any younger, Walter. None of us are.' It seemed easier to

14

put these things by way of a cliché: people took it less personally. And he always liked it when she lumped them together in a thought, casting away her five years' advantage on him.

'I'll be all right, Bren, I'll take care.' Already he was excited by the task, by the thought of being useful once again. The family would try to persuade him to pay for the job to be done, but he would refuse. He could afford it, but that wasn't the point. He would stretch the job over several weeks, working only when the weather was suitable as the year moved through autumn. It would be a prolonged reminder to them all that he was still capable of good work. And the quality of it would be an assertion that he meant to remain in his own house for many years yet.

Brenda Collins read some of this in his face. She said only, 'Promise me that you won't stay up that ladder for too long. Otherwise I'll be worrying about you all day.'

He liked that concern. It was good to have a woman worrying about your welfare. He grinned at her. 'All right, I'll be careful – for you, Brenda. It's almost like being married, this.'

His resolution filled him with restless energy, so that he was suddenly impatient to be away. He began to plan the work, like a campaign. He had the brushes ready at home. He would drive down into Cinderford and get the paint and the creosote today. He took a cheerful and noisy farewell of Brenda at her gate, even more anxious that the news of his visit to her should be relayed to his family, fuelling their speculations about him and Brenda.

She watched him a little longer than usual as he hastened off down the lane. She was more worried about him at the top of that ladder than she had dared to tell him in her house.

As Brenda Collins shook her head ruefully and turned back into the house, another pair of brown eyes followed Walter Fletcher's progress, remaining steadily upon him until he disappeared at the bend in the lane. They were the steady, unblinking eyes of a black Labrador. The eyes

15

knew Walter, but the dog made no effort to follow him.

The dog made no movement at all until its ears pricked at the low command from behind the hedge. Then it turned and loped swiftly away behind its master.

The news got round the family quickly, as Walter had intended it should.

He rang his daughter himself. She was disappointingly philosophical about his plans, when he had expected her to argue with him. 'You must stay at High Beeches if you want to, Dad, of course. I'm sorry you were upset yesterday, but you must accept that everyone meant well.'

She paused, and he knew that she was waiting for a reaction. He pictured her, waiting anxiously by the phone in the bright, modern kitchen where she spent so much of her time in the house. He said grudgingly, 'Perhaps. But they should leave me to make my own decisions. I'll know, when the time comes.' But would he, he wondered. It was the first time that he had even admitted that there might come such a time; it shocked him that he should do so.

Alison said, 'But are you sure it's wise to take on such a big job, Dad? I don't like to think of you up a ladder for all those hours. The eaves of the house are very high.' She was back in her childhood then, looking down the valley to the densest part of the Forest from the window of her small bedroom, a little frightened at the vastness of the world which waited outside, whilst the boys shouted at each other in the room next door.

She said, 'I'd come and give you a hand myself, but they've asked me to work every morning for the next few weeks – until the end of November.'

''taint woman's work, this.' She could hear his satisfaction in that thought. 'I'll be all right, girl. Don't you worry about me.'

She pictured him then as she had been used to see him as a girl, an immensely strong man who worked such long hours that she could remember him only at weekends, moving huge logs around the garden and stopping occasionally to play with the boys.

Sometimes, when the lads' play had been at its most clamorous, he had lifted her high on to his shoulders and she had buried her small fists deep in his thick brown hair, at once scared and delighted as she looked down on the boisterous world below her.

A generation later, she had seen her own daughter Hannah lifted on to those same broad shoulders, with a little more effort and the occasional stagger, her tiny fingers clutching at hair that was still thick but now almost white as she strove to conceal her apprehension. Her father had looked then, she supposed, very much as his son Alan looked now.

She was filled with a sudden sympathy for Alan, who had handled the conversation with his father so clumsily on the previous day. Chris or she should have taken the lead in that; either of them would have been more tactful than Alan. But he was the eldest and physically the strongest, and he had protected the crippled Chris and his little sister Alison from all the childish cruelties of their youth. Old habits die hard, and it had seemed natural to leave him to take the lead in trying to accomplish what they had all wanted.

Poor Alan! He did not have much of a life. He was better off without that bitch he had married, but she was bleeding him dry with her demands for money, so that all his work at the nursery seemed to be just to survive. And Dermot was proving a bad lot: if he went on like this, he would break his father's heart. She felt guilty that she had not done more for her nephew, particularly after his mother had left. But you never knew when Dermot was going to be around nowadays, and he hadn't taken kindly to advice during his adolescence.

She must get round to see Alan soon. They had always been close, but she had neglected him since she had had this exciting new presence in her life.

Alison Fletcher rang her father back later in the day,

feeling a sudden urge to protect him now, as he had protected her all those years ago. But she did not try to change his plans. She said only, 'Do be careful, Dad, when you're doing those gutters.'

Later that night, she waited until her husband had finished marking the school exercise books before she told him about her father's plans. Jim and the old man had never really got on, though there had been long periods of armed neutrality. Yet Jim knew his father-in-law pretty well: he would recognize the plan to paint the outside of the house for the defiant rejection that it was.

Alison thought her husband might erupt into anger at the news. Instead, he sat with his chin in his hands, looking defeated. His thinning hair hung untidily over his left temple, his pinched features twisted a little with his disappointment. After a short silence, he said heavily, 'So he won't be moving out of High Beeches, then. We can forget our plans for a school of our own.'

He did not complain about it; he did not even trouble to condemn her father's plan to paint his house. But Alison wished Jim had expressed some concern for her father. With half-term coming up, he might even have suggested giving the old man a hand with the more difficult parts of the house.

As Walter had intended, the news of his visit to Brenda Collins spread quickly to those he had planned that it should disturb.

At one o'clock, Chris rang him. They had not exchanged ten words before he said, 'I heard you were round at Mrs Collins's house this morning, Dad.'

Walter felt a kind of power that his clever son should have been driven to say this so quickly. It surged through him as he said casually, 'I called for coffee. I quite often do, you know. Nice woman, Bren is.' As far as he could remember, he had never used the diminutive form of her name to Chris before. He enjoyed teasing him with this hint of a new intimacy; after all, Chris was the conversationalist in the family, the one who was supposed to be good with the words. His old brain was a match for younger ones, still.

'I hear you're planning to paint the outside of High Beeches.' Chris waited for confirmation, took the silence at the other end of the line as being just that, and said, 'Are you sure it needs it, Dad?'

Walter was taken aback for a moment. He had been prepared for attempts at dissuasion, but not for the notion that the work might actually be unnecessary. Trust Christopher to take this oblique approach. As if he could be the judge of a practical question like that!

Walter could picture him in the bookshop, sitting back in his armchair with his spectacles halfway down his nose, a mug of tea precisely placed by his elbow, his crippled leg held carefully straight in front of him. Always the intellectual of the family, Chris. Walter was proud of that, even now when he found it irritating him.

'The house needs painting, son. Take it from me, it needs it. But I'll do a good job. Last for years – see me out, perhaps.' He was pleased to offer that thought, with its unspoken suggestion that he would spend the rest of his days in his own house.

His own father had often used that phrase, half jokingly, as Walter did now, and his son recognized it and gave the customary reply. 'You're good for a long time yet, Dad, and you know it. But there must be better ways to occupy yourself.'

'Such as?'

That stopped him in his conversational tracks, as his father had known it would. Chris, looking round the neatly catalogued books on the shelves of his tightly packed shop, knew how he himself would have preferred to pass the time. The theatre, or the film club, or simply reading: all of them would be preferable to being stuck up a ladder for hours on end in the autumn cold.

But his father would see none of these as preferable to physical action and the satisfaction from a physical task

19

performed well. He said, 'Perhaps you should give yourself a holiday. A walking holiday, maybe. What about the Lake District? You used to enjoy that, and it's years since you've been.'

Walter, listening to the desperation in the words, said quietly, 'Ain't been up there since your mother was able to go with me. I don't fancy it on my own, Chris.'

He could hear his son breathing, a little unevenly, as he always did when uncertain of himself. Walter wondered mischievously whether to make some suggestion about Brenda Collins, but his son eventually said lamely, 'Well, just don't embark on the painting too hastily. It's a big thing for you to take on, Dad.'

Typical of Christopher to be so unpractical. If you were going to paint the outside of the house at this time of the year, you needed to get on with it, before autumn turned into winter. Walter told him as much, and rang off quickly. That would reinforce the impression of urgency.

They needn't think there was anything empty about his life.

Later that day, when it was too dark for his brother to be working in the single field he had turned into a smallholding and plant nursery, Chris rang Alan, as Walter had known he would. The two lads had totally different temperaments, but the ties of blood had always kept them close.

Chris said, 'Did you hear about Dad?'

'No. I've been lifting roses all day, ready for the market at Malvern. What's the old bugger done now?' Alan was tired, and still smarting a little from the exchanges with his father on the previous day.

'He's planning to paint the house. Wants us to realize that he intends to stay there, and that he's capable of looking after himself, I suppose.'

'Yes.' Alan resented the implication that he wasn't capable of working these things out for himself. People thought if you worked on the land you were a yokel, like the ones in the leatherbound volumes of *Punch* he had

20

thumbed through in that funny old shop of Chris's.

'And he went round to see Brenda Collins again this morning.' In the face of his brother's silence, Chris felt increasingly like the village gossip. Bachelors living alone became more and more like old maids, he was sure of it. Well, that wouldn't be him for much longer, would it?

He said rather desperately, 'Do you think Dad really is thinking of getting married to her?'

'Not unless he's getting senile in his seventies. He's got more sense, I should have thought.' Alan Fletcher's voice was harsh, but curiously unconvincing. The sentiments came from his own experience rather than from any objective assessment of his father's intentions. Since his own marriage had broken up in acrimony and recriminations, he had become understandably bitter. He now had to maintain an expensive residence in Surrey for the wife he never saw. Women, he invariably implied nowadays, were a dangerous encumbrance which wise men would avoid.

His brother moved off the subject a little too hastily. 'Have you seen Dermot recently?' he said, as casually as he could. Alan's son had officially left with his wife, but he appeared occasionally in the Forest of Dean still. He was twenty-one now; he had rarely been out of trouble since he was fifteen. Three years ago, he had even stolen money from his own grandfather at High Beeches.

You couldn't expect a father to see it, but to Chris's mind, Dermot meant trouble. The less he was seen in the area, the better it would be for his family.

Alan Fletcher was silent for a few long seconds; perhaps, his brother thought, for a little too long. Then he said firmly, 'I'm hoping Dermot will be home with me, you know, when I begin to develop this place. Working alongside me.' There was a pause, and he seemed to realize that he had still not answered his brother's question. He said reluctantly, 'But I've seen very little of him, these last few months.'

3

Walter started work on the house at nine o'clock on the following morning. As he climbed the first rungs of his ladder, he felt a heroic defiance in the action.

That did not last long. He spent the first two hours on the harsh work of preparation. Scrubbing at peeling paint with a wire brush soon removed any sense of heroism from the enterprise. By eleven o'clock he felt very tired and rather ridiculous. His knees trembled a little as he descended the ladder in response to the call for coffee which he had been secretly anticipating for the last twenty minutes.

'Ought to have more sense at your age,' said Eve Brownrigg. She put down the tray on the table in the conservatory and looked at him with her head on one side, as if assessing the state of health of an elderly and unintelligent dog. 'You get someone like me to help around the house, and then you go staggering up ladders. Ought to have more sense, I say.'

The repetition gave her considerable pleasure, as if it was a second and different voice which confirmed her opening opinion. She was a white-haired, vigorous woman who had come in to this house to clean for a quarter of a century. She came on two mornings a week now, often making him a plate of sandwiches as a supplement to her domestic chores before she left.

'It's good for me to do things, Mrs Brownrigg,' Walter said. 'Helps to keep the advancing years at bay.' He found himself more honest with her than he would have been

22

with any of his children. Indeed, he now saw clearly for the first time why he was doing this, and felt a little silly in his stubbornness. He never addressed his cleaner as anything other than 'Mrs Brownrigg', even after all these years. It was a relic of an older system of master-servant relationships, which both of them felt comfortable with because they had known it as children.

Curiously, she felt more licence within this framework of formality than if they had been on first-name terms. 'Daft, that's what it be, if you ask me,' she said.

He almost told her that no one had. But that would have shut her up, and for some reason he did not want to do that. He found her scolding a comfort, he supposed, a reassuring thing in a world that was changing with such disconcerting swiftness. He said, 'If you want a proper job doing, you have to do it yourself, nowadays.'

'Well, there's something in that,' she conceded grudgingly. She had supported an invalid husband for forty years; his wounds had made their full impact only ten years after Hitler's war, which ensured that his pension was tiny, though it had crept upwards after reluctant bureaucratic reviews. They had to pay for maintenance work to be done around their tiny cottage: Eve Brownrigg knew all about modern standards of workmanship and modern prices.

They exchanged a few more comments on Walter's foolishness and the unhelpful world around them. Then the phone rang and she hurried away to answer it, rolling slightly on the bandy legs that were a result of rickets during a childhood in the last years of the thirties depression in the Forest. She had had a hard life, thought Walter. Then he grinned as he heard her telephone voice from the hall saying in lofty tones, '0721. Mr Fletcher's domestic.'

Reluctantly, he eased himself stiffly back to work and climbed carefully up his ladder. A long time seemed to pass before Mrs Brownrigg called up from below him, 'I'm finished now, Mr Fletcher. Don't you be staying up there too long, mind.'

In truth, he had been waiting to hear Eve's farewell for at least half an hour. He waited only until she was out of sight before lowering himself rung by rung and shuffling into the kitchen to wash his hands. He put the radio on and sat down in the armchair by the plate of sandwiches left ready for him on the table.

It was an hour later that the strident jingle at the close of *The World at One* brought him abruptly awake. He must have been more tired by his morning's efforts than he had admitted to himself. Well, it was hard work, the preparation for painting. Had been, even when he was young. He made himself a mug of tea and chewed his sandwiches slowly.

The worst work of the day was over. He had decided before he started to ration the difficult and unrewarding task of rubbing down the old paintwork. This afternoon he was going to creosote the weather-boarding of the gable ends. Easier, and more satisfying; you could cover quite a big area in a couple of hours.

Walter found it, as he had expected, much easier than the work he had done in the morning. You had to be careful not to overload your brush, or the creosote ran down your arm. But you could slap it on without any great discrimination, watching it soak into the dry wood and congratulating yourself as you saw it disappear that this work of preservation was indeed necessary.

You had to move your ladder quite frequently, of course. No sense in stretching out too far and risking losing your balance. He had to extend the double ladder to its fullest length to reach the apex of the gable. He climbed gingerly to the top of it, trying not to worry as the aluminium flexed and the treads swayed alarmingly beneath his tentative feet.

He paused for a moment, getting his breath and his bearings before he began work, pressing himself close to the topmost eaves for a little while before he eased his body cautiously backwards and commenced work. You could see the top of May Hill from up here. It could not be more than three miles to the north, as the crow flew.

It was two or three years since he'd been up there.

Perhaps, when Hannah was home from university at Christmas, he'd persuade her to walk up there with him in the frost. Better still, in the snow, if there was any: he smiled, remembering erratic snowballs from his excited granddaughter when she scarcely came higher than his waist. Had the years really fled so quickly since then?

He pushed his body resolutely back from the ladder and began to use the big paintbrush, in tiny, comic daubs at first, then, as the work absorbed him, in more confident sweeps of the brush. Soon he was at the apex of the gable, his feet almost at the top of the ladder, his free hand grasping the small ornamental post at the top of the eaves.

He did not look down; best not to, whilst he was at this highest point of the work. The sun was still well above the tree-clad rise to the west; he should be able to complete the creosoting at this end of the house before the early darkness closed in. He worked industriously, but not too swiftly. The very fact that no eye would be able to discern from ground level whether or not he had scamped the work up here made him more determined that it should be done thoroughly.

When the base of the ladder slid suddenly sideways, he lost his precarious balance before he even knew what was happening. He clutched, and missed, at the top rung, which was almost touching the boards of the house below him. But his trunk was stiff with the work and the cold, and the rung was just too low for him to reach it.

His fingers brushed it agonizingly. Then he fell backwards, through the thin autumn air. He began a cry, which was more in fear of the next world than of this. The sound was abruptly checked as the back of his head hit the flags at the base of the wall. His body hit the ground with the awful sound of breaking bones.

The blood ran quickly from the head for a time, then

25

slowed to a tiny trickle. It congealed and darkened in a small pool, as if waiting to be inspected by the sightless eyes beside it. By nightfall, yellow leaves had drifted into the grisly puddle, and the blood around them was almost black.

4

At this point in the journey, Hannah always remembered what her grandfather had said when she sat on his knee. It was the very first story she could recall from her childhood.

'When I came home on leave in the war, I always waited for the first sight of May Hill,' he had said. 'I knew then that I was nearly home, you see.' And they had looked together, the ageing man and the toddler with the same bright-blue eyes that he had, at the hill which rose above them. You could see the copse of trees at the summit from any angle and from many miles around.

Now, twenty years later, Hannah waited for her first glimpse of that copse with the same eagerness that the young soldier once had, with the same sense of reassurance that home and all that home meant was at hand. May Hill commanded views of seven counties: Granddad had pointed at each of them in turn with his stick. That had been on her tenth birthday, a day when rain was on its way in from Wales and each ridge of the Black Mountains to the west and the Cotswolds to the north and east had stood out with limpid clarity.

Yet the hill which had once seemed a mountain to her was less than a thousand feet high – Granddad had always refused to translate it into metres, and loyalty demanded that she thought in his terms. Especially now, when she was coming home for his funeral.

'Don't come if you're busy with your studies,' her mother had said on the phone. 'You know Granddad would have understood.' He would, too, she thought, hugging her sports bag to her chest with a sad little smile, as the bus moved over the rise and turned away from May Hill, beginning the descent into the valley where her family waited.

Granddad would have looked past her and said, 'You must get on with your life, m'dear, and not make plans around old fogies like me.' And when he had convinced himself he really meant it, he would have looked her full in the face, and smiled that grave smile of his, where only the twinkling blue eyes hinted at humour. Her own eyes glistened again with the tears she had thought were finished.

They passed the entrance to the lane which led up to the old man's house. It looked deserted, bereft of all human life, as if a whole area had been sealed off with her grandfather's death, instead of just his own house and garden. As indeed it had for her, she thought bleakly; she could not imagine herself taking that well-trodden route to High Beeches again, with no one to greet her at the end of it.

She was glad her mother was in the garden when she got home. There were only two buses a day, so Alison Hargreaves had heard her arrival. The mother looked at her daughter with that old anxiety about her reactions which all mothers seemed to have: Hannah felt her impatience arising at it, even now. She was surprised as well as delighted when her father came round the corner of the house and held out his hands to her.

It must be half-term at his school, of course. She had forgotten about such things when she moved on to the grander world of the university. Jim Hargreaves held his daughter's hands tightly for a moment in his, less obvious in his assessment of her emotions than her mother had been. He clasped her briefly and clumsily against him before he said, 'It's a bad business, this, Hannah. I'm sorry you've had to come home in circumstances like these.'

It was conventional, even stiff, for a father to a daughter, but she did not mind, for she felt his care for her seeping round the words. She said nothing as the three of them moved into the house, not trusting herself to speak without weeping, not wanting to cry again, even here, where it must surely be allowed.

Then her father, wanting to have the thought out and finished with, said abruptly as they stood in the kitchen, 'You can't see him. We had the coffin lid screwed down. It seemed best, you see.'

She thought even at the time that it was a curious way to be received.

Walter Fletcher's funeral took place ten days after his death. The delay was caused by the necessity for an inquest. The Coroner's Court had heard the evidence of the postmortem, listened to the family's account of the old man's plans to paint his house, received the coroner's low-key summary of events and sympathy for the bereaved, and duly pronounced a verdict of 'Accidental Death'.

Walter's mortal remains were disposed of by a burial, rather than a cremation: on this last journey as in other things, he was an unapologetic upholder of tradition. The vicar spoke briefly but movingly of Walter's life and virtues. It was a relief to him to have a funeral in which the central figure had been a regular attender at his ancient church. If there were only more people like Walter Fletcher in his flock, he would not now be servicing three parishes.

He was a young man, but he was wise enough to keep these thoughts to himself whilst he spoke of Walter's steadfast faith, of his service to his country half a century earlier in that desperate world conflict that the young were in danger of forgetting, of his love for his family and the delight he would have taken that they were here today to witness his last short journey.

Walter's granddaughter, looking along the rows of grave faces on the pews beside and in front of her, wondered

29

how much grief there was behind each of these serious, unrevealing faces. A few minutes later, she studied them again at the graveside, so intently that when her turn came to throw damp earth upon the bright plate of the coffin lid in the hole below her, she was not ready for it. She stumbled a little on the plastic grass the diggers had set beside the grave, so that her father caught hastily at her arm and the white faces opposite her looked up in sudden alarm.

They thought, of course, that Hannah was made fragile by her grief: everyone knew how close the old man had been to his granddaughter. Closer, some said, than he had been to his own children. But then love was a strange and unpredictable thing; it often found it easier to jump a generation.

They had a reception at the King's Head in the village for the family and the friends who had known Walter for most of his life in the Forest, of whom there were a surprising number. But perhaps it was not really surprising: Walter had been born at the other end of the valley where he had died, scarcely six miles away, and he had lived in only three houses in his life, all of them within the narrow confines of that quiet green place.

The hum of conversation rose as the tray of wine glasses was depleted. The dark, unfamiliar funeral clothes sat uneasily on the folk of the Forest, who were able to maintain an unnatural formality for only a limited period. By the time they sat informally among friends with their sandwiches and sausage rolls, voices were raised and little outbursts of laughter were beginning to echo around the functions room of the ancient inn.

Hannah, enduring only her second funeral and imbued with the puritanism of youth, felt obscurely that it should not be so. But she was too preoccupied with the idea which had burned in her mind all day to register any very strong distaste for the jollity which gradually displaced solemnity, as reminiscence and anecdotes crept into the conversation.

If she was right, there was someone in this room, someone who had come with solemn face and sorrowing mien to the church, who was inwardly rejoicing in her grandfather's death. She looked at her mother and father, watching the food and drink disappear like anxious hosts. She watched her uncles, Chris, with his damaged leg and gentle, vulnerable face, and Alan, with his ready smile upon the tanned, outdoor features, and tried to find her notion ridiculous.

But of course, it need not have been one of them. There were others here who had had access to her grandfather and might have wished him ill. She looked fondly upon old Eve Brownrigg, already a little tipsy with even a little of the unaccustomed alcohol, but ministering as tenderly as always to the needs of her crippled husband. He sat in his wheelchair with his white hair a little dishevelled, delighted but slightly bewildered by the unaccustomed company and the increasingly boisterous exchanges of the occasion. The woman who had cleaned Walter Fletcher's house for a quarter of a century had surely wished him no ill. But she might know someone who had.

And there were others, not even here, who might know things. Brenda Collins, Hannah realized suddenly, had not come here after the church business was over, though she remembered her standing erect and a little apart from the others at the graveside. And there was one other figure, nearer to her own age, whom she had not seen at all today, who had not even thought it necessary to grace the old man's funeral with his presence, who might have to give an account of himself.

Hannah's home, with its profusion of bright Michaelmas daisies softening the harsh orange of the modern brickwork, was scarcely half a mile from the King's Head. The door from the functions room into the pub garden had been opened on this still autumn afternoon, and she could hear the distant sounds of conviviality as she walked into the silent house. No one had noticed her stealing away from the reception.

31

She found her old bicycle at the back of the garage. It was behind the mower and the garden tools; there were cobwebs tracing their intricate network across the spokes of the front wheel. She wobbled a little uncertainly as she began her journey, but soon steadied herself into something like a rhythm. She rode carefully past the cars parked around the pub and began the climb away from the village.

She stopped on impulse as she passed the lych gate of the now silent churchyard. The brown clay was mounded upon her grandfather's grave. The colours of the flower sprays upon it seemed even brighter in the early twilight. She knew the small spray which was hers, felt no inclination to read the labels upon the other tributes. She stood beside the deserted grave, quietly contemplating the life of the man who was gone, framing a prayer to the God in whom she thought she had ceased to believe, steeling her resolve for what she was determined to do.

Then she rode on, the pedals creaking a little from lack of use, allowing no dimunition of her purpose even as her limbs began to tire with the effort.

It took her forty minutes to reach the place; she was glad to find the lights still worked on the old bike. She knew the road, but she was not sure of the house, so that she had to ask some children on the recreation ground which one it was.

'That's my dad!' a sturdy boy of about ten said proudly when she gave the name. He pointed out the house to her, his football forgotten for a moment beneath his arm. She found his cheerful curiosity a comfort, as if the innocence of childhood insulated her against the dark theory which had brought her here. She was conscious of the children, following her at a respectful distance as she went through the double gates and up the driveway to the house.

A woman, a little younger than she had expected, opened the door to her. In her agitation, Hannah had not considered the possibility that he might not be at home.

But the woman called up the stairs behind her, 'Bert? It's for you.'

He came down the stairs in his shirtsleeves, grey now at the temples, a little more weighty than she remembered him. 'I'm Hannah Hargreaves, Sergeant Hook,' she said, the words tumbling out too hurriedly, as if she feared that at the last minute she would not be able to carry this through. 'You won't remember me, but –'

'I remember you, m'dear,' he said. 'In the sixth form, when I came in to talk about drugs.' He would not have got the name, but he remembered the face. Well, that was part of his training. The fact that it was such a pretty face was just an additional help. 'What can I do for you?'

She was absurdly reassured by his remembering her. She followed him into the lounge, where he picked up the toys from the floor and gestured towards a chair. She spoke breathlessly, scarcely believing that these words came from her. 'It's about my granddad, Walter Fletcher. We buried him this afternoon, you see. Accidental death, they said. But I think he was murdered.'

5

Sergeant Bert Hook reflected that it was just his luck to find Rushton with Lambert. It had been that kind of week, with a puncture on his car and a GBH slipping through their fingers in court when an aggressive defence counsel had made mincemeat of a young DC.

Now, when he wanted a quiet word with the superintendent to discuss this delicate matter, he found young, keen Detective Inspector Rushton already ensconced in the armchair by Lambert's window. The last thing you wanted in these circumstances was a man who played things by the book, who most of the time, in Bert's uncharitable view, could see nothing beyond the book.

John Lambert sensed Hook's discomfort immediately, was even amused by it. On a dull day, there was room for a little byplay between the rubicund but deceptively acute sergeant and the zealous but unimaginative inspector, both of whom were valuable members of his team. 'What can I do for you, Bert? You said you wanted a word.'

Hook almost said he'd come back later. Then he sensed that such a thing would not be allowed. They were, after all, supposed to be working together, as Lambert had reminded both him and the fresh-faced Rushton when their temperaments had clashed in the past. He said, 'It's a tricky one, sir. And it may mean nothing.' He rarely gave Lambert his 'sir' except on public occasions; its use now was a symptom of his unease. They had worked together for eleven years; they knew each other's weaknesses as well as strengths.

All three men were aware of Walter Fletcher's death. Any violent death came to the attention of the CID. When, as in this case, it was legally established that there had been no foul play, that was a matter for relief. Bert took them briefly through the details of Hannah Hargreaves's visit. As he did so, the reasons for opening up any sort of investigation seemed even more flimsy than they had before he had come into the room; he wished again that the attentive Rushton had not been there.

It was Rushton who spoke when Hook finished his account. 'The postmortem report was fairly conclusive. I can get it in two minutes if you want it,' he said to Lambert. Chris Rushton was proud of his computer files, anxious to prove the efficiency of the modern technology he had argued so hard to secure in the Oldford CID section.

Lambert was still looking at Hook. 'Forensic said the injuries were commensurate with an accidental fall from a ladder, Bert. Are you suggesting you can produce something to overturn that?'

Hook said stubbornly, 'Walter Fletcher was killed by a fall from the top of a ladder. That's all that was really established by the PM. No one disputed that. And there was nothing at the time to suggest that anyone else was involved.'

'And now you think there is?' Rushton was unable to keep the scepticism out of his voice.

'I think we should check that we still agree it was accidental, that's all. As informally as possible.'

'But you can't do these things low-key. You know as well as I do that any suggestion of unlawful killing will flash round the area in hours. And we'll have an unsolved crime on our statistics, where until now there was no crime at all.'

Lambert said, 'We have to see justice done, Chris. Even if it means spoiling our monthly clear-up returns.' Not for the first time, he wondered why Rushton so often made him sound in his own ears like the stuffiest of moralizers. He turned back to his sergeant. 'This Hannah Hargreaves. How reliable would you say she was, Bert?'

'I scarcely know her. She seems quite a level-headed young woman, in normal circumstances. When I went into her sixth form a couple of years ago to talk about drugs, she chaired the session. And she helped when we organized the half-marathon for charity. She's at university now, but she remembered me when she wanted to talk to someone about her grandfather. Said I was the only policeman she knew.'

'And she convinced you that the old boy had been murdered?' Again Rushton could not keep a note of incredulity out of his voice.

'Far from it. I just think we should investigate it. Confirm our original thoughts, in all probability.' Hook was calm but stubborn in the face of the younger man's scepticism.

'What made the girl think her grandfather hadn't simply fallen from his ladder?' said Lambert.

Hook chose his words carefully. He had to make the best use of the one fact he had to offer. 'She said he had a method of attaching his ladder to the wall. He'd shown her. He tied it to a drainpipe or a hook, to make sure it wouldn't move. She reckons the ladder couldn't have slipped in the way it's supposed to have done, and the old man couldn't have fallen like that. For what it's worth, I think it had cost her a great effort of will to come to me at all.'

There was a pause before Lambert said, 'It's pretty thin, Bert.'

Rushton, as if he had been waiting for a lead, said, 'And why did none of his family bring this up at the inquest?'

'According to her own account, Hannah was very close to the old man. He told her more about the way he was thinking than he did his own children – he seems to have become rather more isolated from them since his wife died. And of course, if she's right, one of them at least

36

might have a very good reason for concealing such knowledge.'

Lambert pursed his lips, frowning as he took the decision he did not want to take. 'Chris, you assemble the evidence we have, including the full PM report and anything the uniformed men turned up at the time. I'll clear it with the Chief Constable first, but Bert and I will have a quiet look round at the scene of Fletcher's death. Or as quiet as we can.'

He knew already that they would not be welcome visitors.

The Forest of Dean is never a noisy place. Sandwiched between the Severn and the Wye, it is bypassed by the motorway network which forms the throbbing arteries of Britain at the end of the century.

On this afternoon in late October, the area was even more than usually quiet. A hazy sun gave soft illumination to the golds and russets of the leaves. There had been no autumn gales this year, so that the great tracts of deciduous trees still held their full canopies of leaves. Today there was no wind at all, though a few leaves detached themselves and drifted in a gentle reminder of the passing days. With the first frost, the leaves would fall in a steadily descending curtain.

Lambert and Hook drove along the A40 until they were almost beneath the landmark of May Hill, then turned towards the low sun and into the Forest. It should have been a welcome escape from the CID section in the functional but soulless new building in Oldford. Many people would have taken this very route for a pleasure drive; no doubt at weekends many drivers would do just that.

But Lambert, knowing that he was on a journey which might fracture the life of a community, found himself growing more gloomy as the roads narrowed and they met other cars less frequently. When they turned on to the narrow road to the village of Endean, the tree trunks grew at the edge of the tarmac and their branches touched overhead in a light golden framework.

Lambert, sitting beside Hook, wished he was driving himself, so that the concentration could have thrust out his unwelcome reverie. He felt as if he was entering a sinister, folk-tale world, where his movements were followed by unseen, hostile eyes. He had never taken to the brothers Grimm; this felt like the beginning of one of their gloomier tales.

It was all right for Hook, he reflected ungenerously. Bert was a Gloucestershire man, brought up on the fringe of this tight and exclusive Forest world. No doubt he had played cricket round here: he seemed to have delivered his bustling seamers on every village green for a hundred miles around in his twenty-five-year career. But for a man like himself, who had been born in the London blitz and had cut his teeth on urban policing, the narrow valleys of the Forest seemed claustrophobic, casting an atmosphere of brooding suspicion over his every move.

'More sheep than people round here,' said Bert Hook, as he negotiated three pregnant ewes and ran the car into the tiny village of Endean. There were no cars in the car park of the King's Head at half past three in the afternoon. Thin columns of grey smoke rose vertically into the air from the cottages beyond the inn. Though the coal which had provided employment for centuries to the miners of the Forest was almost exhausted now, there were still plenty of open fires in the area, where timber at least was always plentiful.

They turned carefully on to the narrow lane that ran up to the house where Walter Fletcher had died. Lambert reflected that apart from a couple of people in cars, possibly outsiders like themselves, they had not seen a single person since they had left the A40. He had an uncomfortable feeling that several people had seen them.

They found the place easily enough. It had a neat, white-lettered High Beeches sign on the smooth trunk by its five-barred gate. The wood at the top of the high gable end which faced them as they went through that gate had been newly creosoted: eleven days after the death of the workman, the smell still hung faintly about the timber in the noiseless autumn air. The gutters at the corner of the house had been prepared for the paint they had never received; as the sun caught the patches of raw metal, they gleamed like teeth above the two visitors, a grim reminder of the owner's abruptly interrupted purpose.

The last of the sun filtered gently through the tall beeches behind them. One of the flags at the base of the gable wall had been carefully scrubbed, removing the pool of blood which had congealed around the old man's broken head. They rang the bell, as if observing some archaic ritual. The chimes rang hollow within the hall, assuring them that they were alone. Someone had removed the ladder, but they knew what they were seeking.

'If what the girl told me is right, there should be hooks in the wall. According to her, her grandfather fastened his ladder to them when there wasn't a drainpipe handy – tied a bit of rag or a piece of rope around them, to make sure that it wouldn't shift.' Hook wondered why he was whispering: that must surely be unnecessary in this deserted spot.

They found the hooks easily enough, two of them, galvanized, weathered to a dull grey, unobtrusively set between the bricks beneath the level of the weather-boarding above. They were perhaps eight feet above the flags on which they stood.

The first one was clean enough. It was the second one which revealed what was so unwelcome to them. Lambert found a broken chair in the outhouse beyond the locked garage, and climbed gingerly on to it to bring his grey eyes within three inches of what he had seen from below.

It would have been innocent enough, in another con-text. It was no more than three strands of winceyette, probably torn from a working shirt or a pair of discarded pyjamas. He examined them carefully, but did not touch them. He lowered himself stiffly back on to the flags.

He said heavily, 'We'll need to get the Forensic boys back. And set up a Scene-of-Crime team.'

6

Hannah Hargreaves did not look at all like a girl who might have set a murder enquiry in train. She looked to Lambert absurdly young as she sat in the armchair in his office beside the substantial figure of Bert Hook.

She also looked vulnerable. The possibility that she might indeed be at risk troubled both the men who were questioning her. People who revealed murder might well need protecting, especially when the killer had probably been congratulating himself that the crime had not been detected. Protection for Hannah Hargreaves would be difficult to provide: Lambert was uncomfortably aware that the only real protection would be afforded by the swift discovery of the murderer of Walter Fletcher.

'We thought you would prefer to talk to us here than at home,' he said.

She smiled wanly. 'Safer, as well as less embarrassing.'

She knew, then. He was suddenly full of admiration for this slight, earnest figure in the black leggings and thick woollen sweater, who had been so determined to do justice to the old man she had loved. 'The first thing I have to tell you is that your fears about your grandfather's death seem to be wholly justified. Sergeant Hook and I found fibres from an old shirt on one of the hooks you mentioned.'

There was no need to mention the hornet's nest that had been stirred up within the Oldford police headquarters, the questions about the too-easy acceptance of an accidental death, the failure of the original officers at the scene to spot those fibres and thus bring in the CID resources that should have been there from the start.

Hannah said, 'Could it still have been an accident? If Granddad tied the ladder with just a rag, couldn't it just have torn or come unfastened?'

Her face showed that she knew the answer before he spoke. He was a practical man, her grandfather: he would not have been careless like that. Lambert said gently, 'I'm afraid not. We put in a Scene-of-Crime team as soon as we found those fibres. They found the shirt that had tied the ladder under one of the sheds behind the house. It had been cut. The Forensic lab has since matched the fibres and confirmed that.'

The long pale face with the regular, attractive features was abruptly appalled, as if it had needed this kind of detail for her to face the horror of deliberate, planned murder. Or was she facing something more: the knowledge that someone close to her had perpetrated this darkest and foulest of human crimes? 'Why – why didn't the person concerned take the evidence away with them?'

Her brain was still working, then. A shrewd, observant girl. A good witness, if necessary, in due course. Pity she hadn't been around at the time of this death. Though her whereabouts at that hour, like a lot of other things, would need to be checked out over the next few days.

Lambert smiled at her, encouraging her to relax. 'Perhaps you should consider the police force as a career after you've finished your studies. You raise the first query that comes into our minds. It seems curious that a murderer – I'm afraid we now have to think in those terms – should leave a piece of evidence around, though there was a hasty attempt at concealment.'

'Perhaps someone else arrived at the wrong moment.'

'That is one possibility. He – or she – might have been disturbed, though that would indicate that whoever disturbed him also chose not to report your grandfather's death at the time. Or our killer may have been so confident that this death would be presumed to be an accident that he was a little careless. According to the postmortem conducted upon your grandfather's body, it seems probable that he died during daylight; I know he wouldn't have been up the ladder at any other time, but at least the PM confirms the manner of death. So it may simply be that whoever cut that rag from the hook didn't want to be seen with it about him if he was spotted in the area.'

'Or if it was an impulse killing rather than a premeditated one, he might simply have been appalled by what he had done. Perhaps he wasn't thinking straight.' In spite of her horror, Hannah was enthralled by the puzzle, almost against her will.

'All these things, and others too, are possible. There is no reason, for instance, that the killer has to be male.' He watched her eyes widen a little before she gave a sharp little nod. 'It is the business of an investigation to find out such things. And you are an important starting point for us. I want to pick your brains before you get back to the university.'

Where you will hopefully be safer than around here, Lambert thought grimly.

The girl looked at him, blue eyes narrowing a little, suddenly defensive. She looked young, almost childish; yet she was more astute than many people of twice her age. She said, 'I don't know any more than I've told you. I just knew that Granddad had this method of tying his ladder to the wall, to make sure he didn't fall.'

'With respect, you do know other things. Things you don't even think of as important, which may be of use to us.' She was intelligent enough to know that the first suspects would be the family: he could see her face setting already into an uncooperative mask as they arrived at that thought.

Fortunately, the coffee he had ordered when she arrived was brought in at that point. His secretary put the tray on his desk and went straight out, familiar with the hiatus which fell upon exchanges in her presence. Hook handed the girl a cup and saucer, then sugar, milk and biscuits, in his clumsy, tender way. It was a pity he had only two sons, thought Lambert with silent amusement: a daughter would have loved Bert, even during her adolescence.

At the briefest of nods from his chief, Hook took up the questioning. 'You want to see justice done for your grandfather, Hannah. We do too, but we need your help. The fullest and the frankest help you can give us. Don't forget we know virtually nothing about this yet, except the probable manner of his death.'

'And how do you go about finding out more? I don't see how I can help you.' Again her face closed. She pushed a stray strand of dark hair back over her unlined forehead, then bit fiercely into a ginger biscuit, as if the action could strengthen her resolve against them.

'We have a method when investigating unlawful killing. It may seem ponderous, but it is a routine which has proved itself, not just here but all over the world. We start with those nearest to the deceased. The immediate family and close friends. If that produces nothing of note, we move out from there, to a second and wider circle, and then to a third.'

'It could be someone who scarcely knew him. Someone who was after whatever they could get from within the house.'

'It could. Enquiries into that possibility go on alongside what we are doing. There are officers at this minute going round every house in Endean, checking whether anyone was seen near High Beeches on the afternoon of the death. We already know that your grandfather was alive when his cleaner left at around twelve-fifteen on that day. I can also tell you that there is no evidence of a burglary inside the house.'

Hannah Hargreaves said in a low voice, 'You think it's one of the family.'

'We keep an open mind. It's fair to say that so far —'

'You're probably right. I suppose I've known from the start that we might have to face that.' She took a large gulp of her coffee. It seemed that voicing the idea was itself a relief, as if she had cleared a hurdle she had feared without faltering.

Bert Hook hesitated, wondering how much she knew of what had already been set in train. 'I have to ask you this, Hannah. Do you know of anyone who might have wanted your grandfather out of the way? Family or otherwise.'

'No.' The response was immediate, almost before he had phrased the question. As if she knew it was too swift, she said, 'I've thought about that, you see, ever since I decided to come and see you about this.'

Lambert, who had not spoken for several minutes, said, 'I'd like you to put yourself in our position, Hannah. We know nothing about the people closest to your grandfather. We shall find out a lot about them in the next week, even if we upset people. We have to tread on a few corns when there is serious crime, and this is the most serious of all. You can save us time, Hannah. And you can give us a perspective we might not get from anyone else.'

She looked straight into the grey, experienced eyes, wondering how far to trust him, how far to take these men at face value. Pigs, they called them, in her corridor at the hostel, but there were student fashions in these things, as in others.

Abruptly, she smiled. 'You won't find them easy, you know, the Foresters. They stick close together. Like to sort out their own problems, without using outsiders.' She wondered why the sentiment was so familiar, then realized that she was quoting her dead grandfather, almost word for word.

Bert Hook answered her smile with his own. 'But you're one of them yourself, Hannah.'

'I suppose so. But I went to school in Gloucester, and now I'm outside the area altogether, getting a wider perspective. Isn't that one of the things higher education is supposed to give you? Anyway, my father was an incomer. From Nottingham. So I know how things can be. Sometimes I think he's never really been accepted.'

'Not even by your grandfather?'

Bert thought he had moved gently into this most delicate of areas, but she shot a swift look at him, perhaps of resentment, perhaps of something nearer to admiration. 'You might as well know from the beginning. Dad and Granddad didn't get on. Never did, from the start, as far as I can gather.'

'Are you saying they were enemies?'

'They weren't perpetually at each other's throats, if that's what you mean. Most of the time, a stranger might not even have spotted it. Quite civilized with each other – except that hostility within a family can never really be civilized, can it?'

She looked up from the carpet on this last thought, asking them for confirmation, suddenly much younger than her twenty years, innocent despite her perceptions. She'll learn all about the mechanics of deception as she gets further into her life, thought Hook. And in that moment he felt himself diminished by his realism.

'Had they had any recent disagreement?'

Her eyes widened a little as she looked at Hook's open, countryman's face, taking in the full implications of the question. But she did not flare up, telling herself that she had been prepared for this when she came here. 'No, they hadn't quarrelled. And Dad didn't kill Granddad. But I would say that, wouldn't I?' She grinned, happy at anything which would relax her tension. 'Now I sound like that tart who was in that political scandal in the sixties.'

'Mandy Rice-Davies.' Lambert had been involved on the fringes of the Profumo affair, making routine enquiries as a young DC. It did not seem long ago to him; to this girl it was history, as distant as Gladstone or Disraeli. He said, 'We shall check out the movements of both your parents at the time of your grandfather's death. It won't mean that we suspect them any more or any less than anyone else. That's how we proceed, you see. By

46

elimination. Unless, of course, we have anything more tangible to follow up.'

He dangled the bait, hoping that the prospect of diverting the investigation away from her parents might induce her to volunteer knowledge or thoughts about others. Either she had nothing to offer, or she chose to refuse the bait. Instead, she said slowly, 'I can't think it would be anyone in the family. I hope it's someone I don't even know.'

'That's understandable. But tell us about the family. We have to start from there, you see.'

She nodded. 'Three-quarters of all killings are domestic. I don't know where I read that. Is it correct?'

'Approximately correct, yes. Probably even an under-estimate. Why didn't your father get on with his father-in-law?' Lambert was suddenly impatient with her coolness, prepared now to destroy her careful control, if it would give him results.

She shook her head. 'I don't really know the origins of the hostility. It goes back to well before I was born. You'll have to ask Dad. I think Granddad was always suspicious of him because he wasn't a Forester. It sounds silly, but when Granddad was young, not many working folk went beyond Gloucester, and they didn't see many people from other parts of England.' She spoke in tones of wonder, as if she could hardly believe that such things were so recent. Lambert had heard old people in city areas speak of their attitudes to immigrants in the same apologetic tones.

'Did it affect your mother's relationship with her father?'

She thought for a moment, her white brow wrinkling as if she was considering some arcane scientific theory. 'No, I don't think so. It's difficult to tell with Mum. She doesn't show you a lot of what she's thinking.'

There was something more here, Lambert was sure. But he was sure also that she was not going to reveal any more about her parents, and he did not want her to close up about the whole family. He said firmly, 'We need to

47

have your opinions about your other relations, Hannah. In confidence, of course.' He glanced at the sheet in front of him, though he was well aware already of the members of this family. 'Your mother has two brothers, I believe?'

'Uncle Chris and Uncle Alan, yes.'

'Tell us about them. Remembering that we know nothing of them as yet.'

'Alan runs a smallholding and plant nursery.'

'Successfully?'

'Yes, I think so. He works very hard. He's always short of money, but that's because of his – responsibilities.' She hesitated over the word; the feminism she had learned in the last few years was contending with deeper and more confusing ties of blood. 'He has to support his ex-wife.'

'Does she live locally?'

'No. We haven't seen her for years. I can scarcely remember her. But I know Uncle Alan has to provide money for her. From what my parents say, it keeps him poor. He certainly never has any money to spare.' She hesitated, then clamped her lips into a thin line, as if determined to offer them nothing more.

'Did your Uncle Alan get on well with your grandfather?'

'Not on the surface. They had rows, far more openly than Granddad and my father ever did. But I sometimes felt that father and son were very alike in temperament, that they clashed more violently because of it. What I mean is, there was quite a bond between them, underneath the rows. I'm sure Uncle Alan would never have killed Gramps.'

The old word from her childhood slipped out and embarrassed her; she had not meant to use it in this grim context. Lambert was more concerned not to comment on the amateur psychiatry. 'What about your other uncle?'

'Chris? He has a bookshop in Cinderford. Not a very successful one, I think. But it's what he always wanted to do. He knows a lot about books, but I wouldn't think he's a very good businessman.'

Probably she was right. It wasn't the right place for a specialist bookshop, set in the small town in the heart of the Forest, the focus of a working community rather than a tourist centre. 'Does he have a family to support?'

'No. Chris has never married. He's the intellectual of the family. Well, apart from my dad, that is.' She gave them a quick, nervous smile. For a moment, she had fallen into the habit of the rest of the family and thought of her father as an outsider. 'Uncle Chris has been a cripple since he was a child – he drags his left leg. Uses a stick when it's really bad. I don't think he was born like that, but I don't know how it happened. It might have been an illness.'

'Has he ever had a wife?'

'No. As far as I know, there's never been a possibility of that. I doubt whether his shop would support more than one. And Uncle Chris is a bit of a loner, anyway.'

'Any recent disagreements with his father?'

Hannah's forehead wrinkled again. Then she gave a little sigh. 'I gather they all fell out with Granddad to some extent just before he died. They had a family gathering and tried to persuade him to give up his house and go into sheltered accommodation. I wasn't there: if I had been, I don't think there'd have been any open quarrel. He listened to me, when he wouldn't listen to his own children.'

It sounded pompous, an assertion made with the arrogance of youth. Yet her listeners, veterans of domestic warfare by virtue of their trade, believed this slight, earnest young woman. Hook said gently, 'Were some of the family more anxious to move him out of his house than others?'

'No, I don't think so. I told you, I wasn't there, so I wouldn't know, would I?'

Yes, you would. You've already claimed to know deeper things than that, thought Lambert. But the girl's normally revealing face had set again into that determined mask, and he knew they would get no further information from

49

her about that meeting. No matter, they would investigate it with the principals in due course. The girl's attitude made him wonder if one or both of her own parents had been a prime mover in this scheme to move the old man out of his home. Perhaps they had deliberately arranged the meeting at a time when they knew their daughter would not be able to attend.

'Who was at this family gathering? Your mother and father; your uncles, Alan and Chris. Anyone else?'

'No. Just that generation. Granddad's children.' She said it bitterly, with the puritanism of the young about the lapses of their parents.

Lambert said, 'But you were away at university, so you couldn't have attended. Were there any of your contemporaries you think should have been there?'

She looked startled then. For a moment she studied his face, wondering how much they knew. Then she said, 'No. There was no one else.'

'Are you the only grandchild?'

Perhaps after all, she thought, you could not trust the police. They were devious, when it suited them: she was being led on here. Again she wondered how much they already knew, how much they were testing her veracity. Well, she would give them the facts: they could find them soon enough for themselves. Her own opinions were another matter: she would keep them to herself.

She said grudgingly, 'No. Uncle Alan has a son, but he isn't around much. It wouldn't have been appropriate for them to have brought him in.'

'Does he live with his mother?'

'No.' She sought for words to allow her an evasion, then decided it was not possible. She glared first at Lambert and then for a moment at Hook, channelling her resentment of the situation against them. Then she said grudgingly, 'You might as well know, I suppose. Dermot has been in and out of trouble for the last few years. We're almost contemporaries: he's just a year older than me. We were quite close until he was about thirteen. Then things went wrong. He was living with his mother then, but spending all the school holidays with his father. I don't think he's been with either of them for any length of time over the last five or six years.'

'How did he get on with your grandfather?'

'He hadn't seen him much for years. When Dermot was young, Gramps spent quite a lot of time with both of us.' She wouldn't tell them about the money Dermot had taken from his grandfather's house when he was eighteen, nor about the old man's anger and hurt. She owed that much loyalty to Dermot, even now. And it couldn't have any bearing on this business, surely.

'But your cousin came back occasionally to see his father and his grandfather? To see you, perhaps?'

She did not blush; she was not a young woman who suffered from blushing. Aware that she was being probed, she found she wanted to tell them as little as possible about Dermot. She did not hurry her reply, seeking for something to divert them. After a moment, she said, 'I've scarcely seen him for years. I think he perhaps came home to see his dog more than anything else. His father got her for him seven or eight years ago, when he was first giving trouble.'

Hook looked up at her from his notebook, ballpoint pen at the ready. He looked suddenly like the picture of the recording angel which had so frightened her years ago at Sunday School in the Forest, so that she wondered how she could ever have gone to him for help and set this nightmare in train. He said, 'What kind of dog is this?'

'A black Labrador. Not pure-bred, perhaps. Very fond of Dermot. She used to go everywhere with him when he first had her, when he was about fourteen. She still does, when he's around the place. I don't know her name.'

That was a lie, and she didn't know why she had told it. Perhaps she was trying to distance herself from her cousin, in the face of this police interest in his actions. Or perhaps she felt that by withholding one unimportant fact she could make up for her other treacheries to Dermot.

51

They let her go after a few more questions, almost as though they had recognized the lie and known that it signified the end of her cooperation. She refused the offer of a lift home, not wanting her parents to see her entering the village in a police car. She stood blinking for a moment in the sunlight outside the police station in Oldford. The weather seemed altogether too innocent for the nightmare she was just beginning to feel encompassing her.

The detectives she had left realized that she had in fact told them little, merely saving them a modicum of time, pitching them into the centre of the investigation without the usual formal preliminaries. They had known already that the deceased had had three children, would have found out about the family gathering and its arguments. Hannah had cut a few corners for them, no more.

Ironically, it was where Hannah Hargreaves thought she had been most evasive that she proved to have given them something of interest.

Lambert called Rushton in when she had gone, and the three CID men pored through the copious but largely negative findings of the house-to-house and other enquiries around the valley where Walter Fletcher had died.

Lambert said glumly, 'No one seems to have seen anyone around Fletcher's house on the day when he was killed.'

Rushton shook his head sadly, knowing how much police embarrassment a quick solution would save in this case. 'No sightings as yet. Not human ones.' He turned over another page of fax paper.

'What do you mean, not human ones?'

'Oh, it's only the postman. He'd have been as likely as anyone to notice people around High Beeches, but he didn't spot anyone. He was in his little red van, but he delivered at most houses in Endean and the valley that day. He did notice a dog near Fletcher's house. Postmen do notice dogs, of course: they treat them with caution.'

'What kind of dog?' But somehow, both Lambert and

Hook felt they knew before the reply came in Rushton's cool, unexcited tone.

'A black Labrador,' he said. 'Greying a little around the mouth.'

7

Murder investigations have a profound effect on any community. They expose secrets, those of the innocent as well as the guilty, and they set the malicious tongues of rumour to work.

When the centre of an investigation is a village as small as Endean, these effects are much accentuated. In this rural section of the Forest of Dean there had been little movement of population for centuries. The result was a complex network of blood ties and intimate social relationships. These intimacies had their bad side: until around 1950, for instance, the village idiot was a real presence in the life of most people in the Forest rather than the folklore figure he has since become.

The good side was the support the members of such communities gave to each other. Life was hard, and tragedy never further than over the next hill, but help was nearly always at hand when fate dealt its harsher blows at the people who lived here. Folk might know more about each other's business than city dwellers would find tolerable, but the knowledge carried an obligation to help.

Among those who did not feel themselves directly involved, the first reaction to the news that the death of old Walter Fletcher had not after all been accidental was one of delighted interest. There was no liking for official evasions about foul play.

Murder. The people of the valley rolled the word from their lips in hushed tones, savouring its melodrama.

When the large police team accorded to such a crime

moved into Endean and the valley around it, the villagers soon became more fearful of the effects of this business upon their lives. There were more policemen in the valley than its denizens had ever seen before, some of them in uniform, some of them in the suits which passed for plain clothes but which were as noticeable as uniforms in this country setting.

Within a day, the villagers began to look with speculation at Walter Fletcher's family, at Brenda Collins, even at old Eve Brownrigg, Walter's cleaner, who it was said had been the last one to see the old man alive. Even the remotest area is nowadays not proof against the profusion of television crime, factual and fictional. Wasn't the last person known to have seen the victim always the first suspect?

Sympathy for those closest to Walter Fletcher had already transformed itself into conjecture. In a few days, as rumour fed on the few known facts and regurgitated them grossly distorted, it would become suspicion.

Alison Hargreaves, who had been for a week after her father's death the focus of condolence and understanding about his fatal fall, now felt the oppressive weight of the new interest. As she drove her old blue Fiesta slowly through the village, warming its engine as slowly as she would have eased life into an old dog's legs, she felt that every eye was upon her.

As if to reinforce the impression, there appeared in her rear-view mirror two large figures, emerging from the King's Head. They stood on the old cobbled area in front of the pub and gazed after the car. They were still there when she turned the bend two hundred yards down the lane and banished them from her view.

Once, she thought, she had only had to conceal these journeys from Jim. That was easy enough, whilst the school term was on. Now, she might need to keep them secret from other eyes. But she could not put this journey off. She needed to see him.

She felt better when she was outside the valley, driving

between the broad stands of oak, watching carefully for the unpredictable movements of the sheep which the Foresters grazed freely here. On this day, she felt better still when she moved outside the boundaries of the Forest itself. She found herself still checking her mirror for any signs of pursuit as she drove into Monmouth.

He calmed her, as he always could, but it took him longer than usual. She told him what had happened, about the police who seemed suddenly to be everywhere, and about what she feared. He took her through it slowly, a step at a time. His stillness and the rhythm of his questioning were themselves reassurances for her.

When she had finished, he thought for a moment, her hands almost hidden between his much larger ones. Then he stood and pressed her against his chest, feeling the anxiety still in her hands as they pressed against his back, waiting until he felt her fingers relax before he held her away from him. He asked her again the last, useless question. 'You're sure that no one saw you up there on that Tuesday?' How could she be sure of that?

She stiffened a little, but he held her firm, and her hands resumed the gentle kneading of his back. 'Yes,' she said, 'I'm sure. There was no one about.'

'Then you must be all right. So long as you stick to the story you've already told when the CID men follow up. Because they will, you know: it's normal procedure. Don't be thinking they've found anything out because different men come to go over the same ground.'

She pressed him away from her then, wanting to see his face, the face she felt she had been waiting to see for every one of the forty-eight hours since Hannah had told them she had been to the police station to talk about her grandfather's death.

She was a clever girl, her daughter. Much too clever, this time.

Alison smiled up into the broad, serious face, with its bushy eyebrows a little ruffled; that was how she always remembered them. 'It's a help, you being a policeman and knowing about these things,' she said.

'Ex-policeman,' he said automatically.

And he was not sure that it was a help at all. He thought about that for a long time, after she had gone.

Lambert did not like working in the Forest. He decided that as Hook drove between the drifts of golden autumn leaves and the shafts of soft sunlight.

This country was all right for pleasure: he remembered long winter walks with Christine, breasting wooded rises to see the Wye below them and the high, blue-grey hills of Wales beyond. And earlier than that, the infrequent but precious Sunday expeditions with the girls when they were small. He could see his two daughters now, waving the crusts of their sandwiches, half brave and half afraid as the curious sheep came closer; he could almost feel the small human limbs pressing ever harder against his knee, as they sat on the old groundsheet. So many years ago, and yet so close.

But when you came into the Forest to work, to investigate crime, things were different. The instinct of the Forest people was to close ranks against outsiders who pried into their affairs, however justified the cause. He had met the reaction before, and knew he was not good at dealing with it.

Perhaps he allowed himself to become irritated and frustrated too easily. Perhaps the best strategy was the one Bert Hook seemed to use; the sturdy detective sergeant affected not to notice any reluctance to cooperate with him, pressing resolutely ahead and outwardly unruffled. Hook's was a reassuring presence for a man to have at his side.

The cottage occupied by Eve Brownrigg and her husband was not the sort that purveyors of the rural idyll put on their coloured calendars. It was a low brick building, dating only from the early years of the century. Its tiled roof was dotted with patches of grey-green moss, its

57

window-frames had in places capitulated to the rot which attacked wherever painting was neglected for a little too long.

Charlie Brownrigg had seen them inspecting the woodwork as they waited for their knock to be answered at the door. 'Began during the war, that,' he said. 'They couldn't get the paint, I shouldn't wonder.' He spoke as if Hitler's war was five rather than fifty years behind them.

He was a frail, white-haired figure in a wheelchair, his legs thin as a child's beneath the tweed of his clean but aged trousers. The blue eyes above the smooth red cheeks were as sharp and mobile as a bird's. Not many strangers came into his world nowadays; he was determined not to miss any of this occasion.

When Eve Brownrigg came in with the tray, her affection for him was immediately manifest. She rolled slightly on the sort of bowed legs which had ceased to exist after her generation, yet she still gave an impression of bustling competence. She served her husband first, putting the cup of coffee and the flapjack on the plastic tray clipped to the arm of his chair without a word; she knew exactly what he wanted, to the last grain of sugar and the last drop of milk.

Only when he was attended to did she turn to the visitors who so animated him. The two large men sat upright beside each other on the two-seater settee, a little too large for furniture which had always seemed quite adequate, a little too formal for a room which had not treated any visitor formally for forty years. They looked to their unwilling hostess a little ridiculous, and thus not at all frightening, though she could not remember speaking to a policeman in the quarter of a century since Endean had lost its own bobby.

As Lambert wondered where to begin, it was the crippled man, his pain-furrowed face alive with the enthusiasm of a schoolboy, who solved the problem. 'She was very good to old Walter, was Eve,' he said. 'Never counted the hours or the minutes, when she was doing that house of his.' In Charlie Brownrigg's mind, the pleasant detached house at the top of the valley, which he had not seen for over thirty years, had become a mansion, his wife the mistress of its domestic arrangements rather than an occasional cleaner.

'He was good to us, Charlie, was Mr Fletcher.' She turned to her visitors as she spoke, sitting down in the chair opposite her husband. 'Always had my money ready for me at the end of the week, without fail. And always in cash.'

Lambert understood. Cheques were difficult when you had no car; probably Eve Brownrigg did not even have a bank account. He said, 'How often did you go up to High Beeches, Mrs Brownrigg?'

'Twice a week. I started going on Fridays when Mrs Fletcher was ailing. After she'd gone, Mr Fletcher asked me to go in more often. I could go three times if I wanted, but twice was enough to keep up with the place. Only one man to make a mess, you see.' She looked affectionately at her husband and he gave a delighted squawk at the sally, avoiding spillage of his coffee with the practised expertise of his long-time immobility.

'And did you go always at the same times?'

'Tuesday and Friday mornings, yes.'

'We shall miss the money,' said her husband suddenly, his concern bursting through the reticence they had agreed on only an hour earlier.

'Hush, Charlie,' she said, as soothing as if he were a child. 'Us'll be all right, and you know it.'

He looked as if he were going to react to that, but she held his excited blue eyes steady against her grey ones for a moment, until he relaxed and nodded. She watched him until she was certain she had quietened him, then turned back to the two men on the couch, suddenly querulous. 'I've told all this to the lad who came round yesterday, you know.'

'Yes, I know, but we have to be thorough. We need

your help, you see. You seem to have been the last person to see Walter Fletcher alive.'

'Except for the one who killed him, it now seems.'

She was no fool, this ageing woman with the tight grey curls and the work-worn but still vigorous body. And she had not ruled out a woman as the killer; most people automatically assumed that homicide was a male monopoly. Lambert smiled at her. 'Exactly so. And you may be able to help us to identify that person.'

She was not at all mollified. It made them wonder what her husband might have said if she had not intervened so promptly. It had been when money was touched upon that she had bridled. Love, lust and money; one or more of them, they said, was behind every murder. And sometimes, Lambert thought, hate, though there seemed none of that here.

As if to reinforce the thought, Eve Brownrigg repeated, 'He was kind to us, was Mr Fletcher. Thoughtful, when others forgot about us.' There might be a wealth of suffering behind that last phrase, but the CID were not here as social workers. Lambert wondered why she so consistently referred to the dead man as 'Mr Fletcher'. Was she concealing a more intimate relationship, or merely preserving the employer-employee relationships of an older generation?

'What time did you leave High Beeches on the day when Mr Fletcher died?'

'Twelve-fifteen. Maybe a minute later than that, but no more.' He looked a question at the precision of this, and she said, 'I can tell from the time I got back here. *Quote Unquote* had just started on the radio. That's on at twelve-twenty-five. Charlie likes to listen to it while I'm getting our dinner. Big reader, you know, is Charlie.' She looked at her husband for confirmation, and the unnaturally red face nodded vigorously, delighted to be so unexpectedly involved in her account.

'Did you see anyone whilst you were up there that

morning? Or on your way to and from the house? It may be very important, as you must realize now.'

'No. I've thought about it a lot. I saw young Albert Jackson, the postman, when he delivered the letters up there. Mr Fletcher gets more than we do.' She didn't seem to notice the lapse in tense.

'What time would that be?'

'He was later than usual. On account of his junk mail, he said. Lot of *Reader's Digest* stuff that day.' She sniffed derisively. 'Must have been eleven o'clock or so, because Mr Fletcher and me, we'd 'ad our coffee.' A thought occurred to her. 'You'll need to ask young Albert. He might have seen someone somewhere in the lanes that morning.'

Lambert smiled. 'Young Albert' must have been nearly fifty. 'We already have, Mrs Brownrigg. Like you, he didn't see anything unusual.'

Except a dog. But there was no need to tell Eve Brownrigg about that.

Hook, who was making notes of anything of interest, had very little on his page as yet. He said, 'Was Mr Fletcher working up the ladder during that Tuesday morning?'

'Yes. With a wire brush. Scrubbing away at the gutters and the paintwork on the windows. Working far too hard, he was.'

'You saw him?'

''Course I did.' She was not so polite to this lesser representative of the law. 'Not for long, mind. I only went out to tell him that his coffee was ready. He looked ready for it, I can tell you.' Her lined, aggressive face softened with compassion at the remembrance.

'And did you happen to notice if he had attached the ladder to the wall in any way? For safety, I mean.'

''Course 'e did. 'e wasn't no fool, wasn't Mr Fletcher. 'e 'ad the ladder tied round a drainpipe with a rag. Where there wasn't a drainpipe near, 'e 'ad hooks in the wall.'

'But you didn't tell this to anyone earlier, did you? When he was first found dead, I mean.'

Hook led her as gently as a child, but she responded angrily. 'No one asked me, did they? I was just told he'd fallen off his ladder and killed himself. You can, can't you? You only have to get dizzy up there and you're gone.'

It was easy to see how things had been overlooked. Eve Brownrigg had not seen the corpse lying up there in its pool of blood; when she heard of the death, she would naturally have presumed that the ladder was still attached to the wall. Accidental death.

'The next question is the most serious one of all, Mrs Brownrigg. Do you know anyone, in his family or outside it, who had reason to wish Walter Fletcher dead?'

She looked at her husband quickly. His eyes were bright, expectant, but it was impossible to be sure whether anything passed between them. Perhaps someone who had known them for years might have spotted some sign of communication, but neither of the pairs of trained, professional eyes which watched them could be certain of it. She said, 'We've thought about that, since your constable came and took my statement yesterday. Most of the family will gain in some way, I expect. He was quite a rich man, Mr Fletcher.'

This time she did glance at her husband, and he returned her look of complicity: they were sure of it. But as she turned back to the two men beside her on the settee, her features fell into a carefully composed blankness. 'But that doesn't mean that any of them killed him. They had their differences, some of them a bit fierce, but I'm sure none of them would have killed him like that.'

'Or in any other way,' said her husband. The little cackle of laughter with which he followed his jest seemed to run round the small, quiet room, tinkling off the brasses on the mantelpiece above his head.

Lambert said gently, 'Could you tell us something about these disagreements, Mrs Brownrigg? What were they about?'

'Oh, family matters. I don't know what.'

She knew more than that, he was sure, but she clearly

wasn't going to tell. Not yet, anyway. He might need to come back when he had seen others and had a fuller picture.

'Do you know anyone else, from outside the family, who might have gained by his death?'

For a moment she looked frightened; he could not quite understand why. Perhaps it was on account of what she was going to say. People in murder investigations were often seized by a belated realization of the implications for others of what they had to tell. He said, more to fill the gap and encourage her than anything, 'Whatever you say will be treated in confidence.'

She looked at him, her face now alive with conflicting emotions. 'There is another woman.'

What a variety of situations that phrase covered! Lambert had heard it a hundred times, in a dozen different contexts. Often it said more about the person who broached the idea than the people concerned.

Eve Brownrigg brought his attention back to this case abruptly with her next words. 'You should talk to Hannah, Mr Fletcher's granddaughter, you know. She was closer to him than anyone. Perhaps she could tell you about Brenda Collins.'

The elderly face twitched as she produced the name. There was jealousy there certainly. Perhaps she was merely possessive about the man for whom she had worked for so many years; perhaps she had nursed a secret, unspoken passion; perhaps there had really been something between the old widower and this domestic help who referred to him so scrupulously as 'Mr Fletcher'.

Lambert said, 'You're saying Walter Fletcher had some kind of association with Mrs Collins.'

She nodded dumbly, concerned now by what she had done. On the other side of the fireplace, Charlie Brownrigg's face was puzzled, even a little hurt. They had plainly not discussed this name between them.

In his large, round hand, Bert Hook wrote the name Brenda Collins in capitals at the bottom of his page.

8

Alan Fletcher watched the small, battered van turn between the gateposts and ease itself over the uneven stones which had once been a farmyard. Chris had driven that vehicle for as long as he could remember: it was now over twenty years old.

Alan came out of the long greenhouse where he had been disbudding chrysanths and said to his brother, 'Old banger's still going, then? Time you were thinking of something newer, isn't it?' Immediately he wished he hadn't said it: it was tactless. The words had come from nervousness, which had made him search for something to say.

But there shouldn't be that sort of awkwardness between brothers. This business was coming between them, as he had known from the start that it would.

Chris Fletcher looked at his van for a moment. He supposed it would soon be time for its annual clean. 'The old girl's still trundling along. She does the job I need; I don't do much mileage, you know.' He tried to feel an affection for the ageing vehicle, as he knew many people did for machinery which they had used for years; he and the van had been through a lot together, after all, and it hadn't often let him down. But he felt nothing for mechanical things, beyond the comfortable familiarity of a man who hated change.

The books he collected and carried within the van, now they were a different matter. He got a real pleasure, almost a sensuous one, just from handling some of them, from

64

turning thin pages with his careful, delicate hands. He could scarcely bear to part with the most beautiful and the rarest of them, though sometimes you had to, to survive.

'You'll be able to buy yourself a new van soon enough, now,' said Alan. The words introduced what they were meeting for, as he had intended, but they sounded blunt and insensitive, even in his own ears. He wondered why he blundered so often into clumsy phrases. Perhaps he had grown too used to dealing with soil and plants, though he had not yet followed his future monarch in talking to them – except to curse them a little when they were particularly intransigent.

Chris looked at him sharply, as he had done so often all those years ago when they were boys and he had suspected his elder brother of trying to put one over on him. Though he was two years older than Chris, Alan had rarely succeeded in deceiving him about anything. But perhaps that had helped their relationship as adults: they had remained close, even as they went their separate ways in life.

It was warm in the big old living-kitchen. The kettle was on the Aga, and Alan had the two mugs of instant coffee made in a moment. Chris said, 'Is Alison coming?'

Alan shook his head. 'She had to go into Monmouth, she said. Some appointment she couldn't break. Hairdresser's, I should think.' He grinned, and for a moment the brothers were back in the old house at the top of the valley with their parents, patronizing the incurable triviality of female concerns.

Chris's smile didn't last. 'I can't stay long. I've got someone keeping an eye on the shop.' The wife of the chemist three doors away, to be precise, who knew nothing about books. She was unlikely to be called upon for any expertise on this weekday morning in October, but Chris would not admit that, even to himself.

'All right. Thank you for coming.' Alan was more nervous than he had expected, and it came out in the formality of his words. This man was his brother, not a casual acquaintance doing him a favour by his presence. He looked automatically at the big round clock over the sink. 'This shouldn't take long. I just thought we should get together. Those of us who were at that family gathering, just before Dad died.'

'Now that we've got ourselves involved in a murder enquiry, you mean?'

Alan looked up quickly at his brother's face, searching for the mockery he had felt in the words: Chris had always been able to make fun of him whenever he felt like it. But there was no hint of humour in the thin, delicate features. Chris's blue eyes met his with the gravity due to his words. 'But you didn't think we should include Jim Hargreaves.'

'He couldn't be here at this time. He's working at the school.' Alan answered too quickly. He was as aware as Chris that that wasn't the real reason. 'I thought Alison could speak for the two of them, anyway.'

'If she was here she could. You're a bit like Dad – perhaps we all are, a little. You didn't think of bringing Jim into the conference because he isn't a Forester. But he was at the family gathering at High Beeches, and he wanted Dad to move out of his house just as much as we did, I suspect.'

Alan did not want to be sidetracked now, particularly by a taunt which was justified. He shrugged his big shoulders against the back of his chair and said, 'I expect you've already had a copper round to take a statement.'

'Yes. And we shall all have more important visitors before long, from the CID.'

Alan didn't question it. Chris seemed always to know about these things. 'That's what I wanted to talk about. We need to put our heads together.'

'Make sure we tell the same story, you mean?'

Alan was shocked at the directness of it. Yet it was exactly what he had meant; he had merely not expected Chris to come straight out with it like that. As though he

66

felt they had something to hide. 'We're all going to benefit from Dad's death. Financially, I mean.'

'Substantially. And none too soon, I'd say, in some cases.' He looked automatically round the room, with its scrubbed deal table and its worn stand chairs, the cracked tiles in the old hearth. Yet he had not meant to imply any insult to his brother; he had been thinking of himself. 'The bookshop needs funds. Quite urgently, actually.'

Alan smiled at his brother's abstracted face with sudden affection. The shop had never really paid, for as long as Chris had struggled with it. It was a labour of love, but an unfruitful one. The shop would never have supported a family; it was well that its single worker had simple tastes. Alan said, 'This place needs an infusion of capital, too.' His bank manager had used that phrase; soon he would be able to surprise that patronizing young face by quoting the words back at him. 'I need more glass, and replacement machinery. Another field, even. And you're not the only one who could use a new vehicle.'

Chris said, 'They'll find out, you know, the police. About what we've all been left by Dad, I mean. People have to tell them things, once it's a murder investigation. Even lawyers. They may already know.'

'I realize that. That's why I thought we should get together.'

'What exactly are you proposing we should do?'

Alan wasn't sure of the detail. He had hoped vaguely that Chris would have been coming up with ideas of his own by this stage. 'I – I'm not suggesting that we should lie to the police.'

So he too had things to hide, thought Chris. Sturdy, straightforward Alan. It was a consolation, in a way. He had thought he was the only one at risk. He said cautiously, 'It would be most unwise to lie.'

'Yes, I realize that.' But there will be some things I need to lie about, thought Alan. But I can't discuss them, even with Chris.

Chris studied him curiously for a long moment, then

said abruptly, 'Is it Dermot, Alan? Because if it is —'

'No. Dermot didn't have anything to do with this. I don't want anyone even suggesting that he did.' Alan's face set into the sullen mask which had become familiar to all of the family over the last few years as his son had got into deeper and deeper trouble.

Chris said, 'We shouldn't lie about our movements at the time of the murder. And we shouldn't put up a united front too obviously. We all stand to gain, and we don't want the police suspecting a family plot.'

Alan was surprised, not by the idea, but by the fact that his brother should be so definite in this assertion. Chris had clearly been thinking about tactics just as much as he had. Did even he have secrets? Abstracted, unworldly Chris?

Alan said, accepting this leadership, 'What are you suggesting we do, then?'

Chris said with scarcely a pause, 'Confer with each other. Make sure after they have been to see us that we are not contradicting each other. They like to divide and rule, when they can. We should all be aware of what the others have said. That way, we may be able to support each other.'

Chris Fletcher became quite animated, began to enlarge a little on his ideas. Alan was glad they had met, sorry only that Alison wasn't with them to join in and be briefed. It was a relief to find they were so much in agreement, to have the initiative for their strategy taken in the end out of his hands.

He watched Chris's van turn into the lane, stood listening to the departing note of its old engine until it was long out of sight. He felt cheered when he went back into the long glasshouse and resumed his work on the chrysanthemums. For the first time since he had heard of his niece Hannah's contacting the police, the musky scent of the leaves and the rhythms of the repetitious work began to bring about their therapy for him.

These blooms were for the Christmas market. All this business might be safely behind them by then.

There were lawyers in the small industrial towns of the Forest of Dean, but Walter Fletcher, staunch bastion of local pride, had chosen to ignore them when making his will. Perhaps the great edifice of English law had drawn a grudging obeisance, even from him, so that he thought the disposition of his property demanded a national rather than a local agency. Perhaps he had merely feared that the confidentiality of his arrangements might be breached if he kept them within the tight world he knew so well.

Whatever the reasons, he had moved just outside the Forest to make his will. It meant that Lambert had only to make the short journey from his office to the centre of Oldford to find out the details of Walter Fletcher's will. It also meant he had to endure the formidable prolixity of the firm's principal, Alfred Arkwright.

It was four years since he had last sat with Hook in the great man's office – he wondered if Arkwright thought of it as chambers. The silver-haired solicitor seemed not to have aged by a single day. And his pastiche of lofty Victorian discretion was in excellent order.

He waved them to the only two seats in the room, other than his own, as though inviting them to select from hundreds, steepled his fingers, and pronounced, 'As always, we are only too anxious to assist the police in the performance of their sometimes distasteful duties. However, you will understand that our professional code dictates that –'

'This is now a murder enquiry, Mr Arkwright. We shall be expecting the usual cooperation.'

'Ah!' Arkwright poured a welter of legal consideration into that long-drawn syllable. Then he accepted the inevitable, but only with an air of an immense concession. 'You shall have our fullest cooperation, of course. However distressing the circumstances, we know where our duty lies.

69

If you will excuse me for a moment, I shall retrieve the relevant documentation from our strongroom.'

Hook had told him the exact circumstances of their visit when he made the appointment, and the will was probably waiting in that outer office where a secretary's fingers fluttered discreetly over her computer, but the forms were being observed.

Lambert whispered when they were alone, 'Didn't I tell you? Polonius to a T.'

'Let's hope he gets stabbed through the arras in due course,' said Hook with gusto.

'That Open University course may have made you aware of Shakespeare at last, but do you have to see every situation in terms of sitcom smut?' said his superintendent, with a mime of distaste.

'Great man for his smut, old William was,' said Bert with relish.

Before he could enlarge on the theme of bardic bawdry, Arkwright was back with them on silent feet. He sat down at his desk and opened up the file he had brought with him, turning to the details of the will he had studied in the half hour before they arrived. 'The last will and testament of Walter John Fletcher,' he intoned sonorously. 'Given at my hand on this fifteenth day of —'

'Mr Arkwright,' said Lambert firmly, 'we have limited time and many people to see. And we are not paying you for this consultation. If you could summarize the important bequests in the will, it would be in the interests of all of us.'

Alfred Arkwright had winced as though stabbed with a flick-knife at the mention of money. He now returned his eyes from the ceiling to the rounded features of Detective Sergeant Hook, but found that the man seemed to be positively enjoying his superior's impertinence. The police, like the professions, were clearly having difficulty in securing the right quality in their recruitment these days. Arkwright sighed. 'I had every intention of revealing all the information you require in due course.'

Lambert said nothing. Hook flicked his notepad to a blank page. Both pairs of eyes waited expectantly. Arkwright, given no words with which to initiate a conversational rally, capitulated. 'The total estate will be valued at something around five hundred and eighty thousand pounds for probate purposes.'

Arkwright expected shock, would even have been gratified for once by vulgar whistles of amazement, but they evinced no reaction. These men were practised in the art of non-surprise lawyers strove so hard to develop. Arkwright had to express the appropriate reaction himself. 'It is a much larger sum, I am led to believe, than most of the people in contact with Mr Fletcher would have expected.'

'And who led you to believe that?' said Lambert impassively.

That ruffled Arkwright; he was not used to his circumlocutions being taken up in this way. 'I – I think it was Mr Fletcher himself. Yes – yes, I'm sure it was, at the time he drafted his will with me.'

'Which was when?'

Arkwright glanced down at the parchment before him. 'Almost exactly two years ago.'

'And what important changes were made from his previous will at that time?'

Arkwright prepared to flutter, but Lambert held up a restraining hand before he could get a decent palpitation under way. 'You are experienced enough to know that any changes are bound to be of interest to us.'

Arkwright said sulkily, 'There were no very significant changes. The two grandchildren were given a rather larger portion of the residual estate; ten per cent each, provided they had reached the age of twenty-one. The remainder was to be divided equally between Mr Fletcher's three children, Alan, Christopher and Alison.' He was ruffled enough to forget to recite the full catalogue of forenames.

'You said the residual estate.'

Arkwright permitted himself a small smile. Wills provided the few moments of drama in a pleasingly ordered life. This was not as promising a moment as those when he revealed the facts of their inheritance to anxious relatives, but he would make the best of it. 'There were certain other relatively small bequests. As these constituted lump sums, they are deducted from the total value of the estate before it is divided among the main legatees.' He rather enjoyed lecturing these impatient men as though they were of strictly limited intelligence and experience.

Lambert said evenly, 'Tell us the exact details of these lump sums, please, Mr Arkwright.' He had always had a sneaking regard for Polonius: now he understood exactly why his creator had brought him to such a sudden and violent end.

Arkwright looked at him for a moment over his gold-rimmed half-moon glasses, then adjusted them unhurriedly to read the relevant clauses in the will. 'There are bequests of one thousand pounds each to the parish church of St Stephen in Endean, to the Royal British Legion, and to the Royal Commonwealth Society for the Blind.' He paused and looked at them over his glasses, pretending to await a reaction from the CID to these momentous revelations.

When they remained resolutely silent, he said, 'There were two other lump-sum bequests. Not large in proportion to the total value of the estate, but substantial enough in themselves to be of some significance.' He looked up at them again, read a warning sign in Lambert's stressed features, and went on, 'The first of these was ten thousand pounds to Eve Brownrigg.'

This time he had a reaction, in so far as he caught the two detectives glancing at each other. Both of them felt gratified, then irritated. The sum was enough to make a huge difference to the lives of people who had as little to spare as the Brownriggs. But it brought them into the frame as suspects, where they might otherwise have been merely useful commentators on the circumstances of Walter Fletcher's death.

Arkwright was perhaps a frustrated barrister. At any

72

rate, he had enough of the legal ham in him to save his most interesting lines for a climax. He said, 'The final lump-sum bequest is in the sum of twenty thousand pounds.' He looked at them again over his glasses, as if making sure that he still had the attention of children, whose concentration might be expected to stray. 'That sum is left to what the testament calls, "my long-time reliable and trusted friend, Mrs Brenda Collins".'

It was the second time that day that the name had been thrown unexpectedly at them.

9

'I thought family murders were easily solved,' complained Bert Hook. 'There's supposed to be an obvious culprit and an arrest within twenty-four hours.'

'And usually a fractured relationship between victim and killer and a conveniently swift confession,' agreed Lambert. 'In this case, we can't even be sure it's a family murder. Many people have killed for smaller sums than ten thousand pounds.'

They were silent then, thinking of the Brownriggs and their windfall, of the mysterious Brenda Collins, whom they had still to meet, of that perennial problem of detection, discovering the minds and passions of people who were complete strangers to them.

They were driving through the Forest in Lambert's old Vauxhall, its engine purring smoothly as he took it around the bends of the lanes. The air was as still as ever, but the sun had gone and the ceiling of grey cloud was oppressively low. There was a hint of damp in the air, and the Forest sheep clustered in small groups to watch them go by. Lambert experienced again that feeling of entering a closed local world, which held its secrets jealously and would resist all attempts by outsiders to discover them.

The impression was reinforced after they turned off the main road and wound two miles on the narrow lane to reach the small village of Endean. Here heads turned to follow them, as men digging vegetable gardens and women coming out of the single village shop spotted strangers. It irritated Lambert, who had deliberately come here in his own car rather than a police vehicle to avoid such interest.

This was a small enough community, sufficiently off the beaten track, for any strange vehicle to be a subject of speculation among the locals. Yet no one had noticed any unexpected person or vehicle around the house of Walter Fletcher on the afternoon he had been killed. Or were the villagers merely keeping such information within their own closed circle?

Alison and Jim Hargreaves were waiting for them in the lounge of their neat modern house, which was within two hundred yards of the church and pub which marked the centre of the village. They had a tray ready with cups and saucers and a plate of scones covered by a paper serviette. Metaphorically as well as literally, man and wife sat on the edge of their seats. Lambert wondered if they had even put on formal clothes for the interview.

Jim Hargreaves had on a neat dark-blue suit with a maroon tie. There was a faint scent of dry-cleaning as he reached awkwardly across them to hand out the small plates and scones at his wife's request. They might have been distinguished but slightly unwelcome visitors who had to be stiffly entertained, rather than detectives investigating a murder.

Neither Lambert nor Hook was surprised. They had met much stranger reactions than this to their efforts, among the innocent as much, or more, than the guilty. Lambert tried to keep any note of irony out of his voice as he said, 'We are indebted to your daughter Hannah for drawing certain things to our attention. Without her, I fear that none of us would today have been involved in a murder enquiry.'

The Hargreaves spoke almost together.

'She's a bright girl, Hannah,' said Jim.

'She was closer to Dad than any of us,' said his wife. The statements overlapped, almost comically, had the circumstances been different. The Hargreaves looked at each other for a moment. Then Alison turned back to Lambert and said, perhaps thinking he hadn't caught her first words, 'He seemed to find it easier to talk to Hannah than to any of us.'

Lambert wondered how far the 'us' ran. Did it include merely Walter Fletcher's three children, or stretch beyond the immediate family? How lonely and isolated had this murder victim been? He said, 'Did you know that Mr Fletcher was in the habit of attaching his ladder to the wall when he used it?'

The question was addressed to both of them, but she took it upon herself to answer without needing her husband. 'No. Perhaps we should have done, but we didn't. Dad was sensible about practical things, so you might have expected it. But he didn't use a ladder very often, I suppose, over these last few years.'

Yet young Hannah, a student probably uninterested in practical things, knew exactly how the old man had proceeded. That was possible, given the propensity of intimacy to skip generations in a family: Hannah Hargreaves herself had suggested that Walter Fletcher had sometimes seemed closer to his granddaughter than to his own children. But it was just as likely that one or both of these two had known about the old man's precautions with the ladder.

Lambert nodded at Hook, who said, as evenly as if he were reading the words from a book, 'The postmortem confirms what we have pieced together from other statements, including your own. Mr Fletcher died between two and four on the afternoon of the twenty-third of October. We cannot as yet be any more precise than that. Perhaps only the person who committed this crime could be more precise. We now need to confirm the details of your whereabouts on that afternoon.'

This time Jim Hargreaves spoke first. He said almost eagerly, 'That's easy enough in my case. I was in the Forest of Dean Secondary School, where I teach.' He smiled a little as he rolled out the name of the school, as if conscious that a roll of eight hundred pupils provided him with a better alibi than most suspects could raise for themselves.

Hook said, taking a little of the wind from Hargreaves's bellying sails, 'That is gratifying. The more people we can eliminate from the enquiry, the easier our job becomes, you see. Were you in the school for the whole of the afternoon?'

'I was.'

Hook made a careful note in his notebook. It did not rule Hargreaves out as an accessory, of course. Already it appeared that there was a high possibility that there had been complicity in this murder; it was a death that was convenient for too many people. It seemed a long time in the still room before the sergeant raised his round face and said simply, 'Mrs Hargreaves?'

'I went into Gloucester. To Sainsbury's, to do the weekly shopping. In Northgate, it is. I left at about quarter to two and was back by about four-thirty.'

It was delivered rapidly, nervously, with her eyes staring straight ahead, but above the heads of the two men who had come here to question her. It had the ring of a state-ment which had been prepared and rehearsed. As if she realized that, she said, 'I've said all this before, to the man you sent round yesterday.'

But she struck the wrong note, to Bert Hook's mind. Irritability would have been understandable, but she man-aged to sound apologetic, as if trying to account for the unconvincing tone of her statement. He said, 'Did anyone from the village go with you?'

'No. I often go with my friend Pat Rogers, but I went on a different day that week.'

'Why was that?'

She brushed a nonexistent straying lock away from her forehead, as if she fancied that it had escaped from the helmet of her neatly cut short hair. This time Alison Hargreaves was flustered, and everyone in the room knew it. It was plainly not a question she had expected. Yet Hook knew that any variation in normal behaviour patterns could be significant in a killing of this sort. Eventually she said, 'I can't remember now. Probably there was some reason why I couldn't go on Friday, as I normally do with Pat.'

'If you think of the reason why you decided to go on that day, perhaps you could let us know. Can anyone confirm your presence in Gloucester on that afternoon?'

She shook her head, a little too quickly, almost before he had completed his question. 'I doubt it. You could try the check-out girls at Sainsbury's, but I doubt whether they would remember me.'

'I doubt it too.' Hook allowed himself a small smile, without taking his eyes from her face. 'Did you go to any other, smaller shops?'

This time she did pause, giving herself time to think. 'I don't think so. If I did, I've forgotten. Oh, I got myself a sweater from Marks and Spencer's. It's still upstairs in its bag, I think.'

'I see. Would you mind if we took it away? It might help us to check your story, you see. Obviously you'd prefer it if we could eliminate you properly from the enquiry.'

'Good old Bert!' thought Lambert. Hook had delivered the line with the air of a servant of the public who was only too anxious to help in these distressing circum-stances. Probably the cardigan would tell them nothing, but it turned the screw a little further on a suspect who was plainly trying to deceive them. Every detective must have a streak of the hunter to be successful. And the woman could hardly refuse a request couched in such reasonable terms.

Alison did not. She looked at Hook for a moment with widening eyes, then rose and left them without a word. Lambert noted that she had not looked to her husband for support throughout her account of her movements, though the pair had seemed prepared to present a united front when the exchanges began. Jim Hargreaves sat look-ing at the carpet in front of him throughout her absence.

Alison Hargreaves was away for no more than thirty seconds, though to her husband they stretched much longer. She came back with a polythene bag with the familiar 'St Michael' label and a dark-green sweater still within it. She held on to it with both hands as she offered it for Hook's inspection. But Bert took it firmly from her with scarcely a glance. 'Thank you,' he said. 'You're sure you bought this on the day when your father was killed?'

'Yes. Quite sure. I don't seem to have kept the receipt, but I know I bought it on that Tuesday.'

Lambert watched her as she relinquished the cardigan. She moved stiffly, like a bad actress on a stage move; her hands lingered limply in the air for a moment after Hook had taken the package from her. Then Lambert said, 'I should tell you that we know the details of your father's will, Mrs Hargreaves. That is quite usual in cases of this sort.'

Jim Hargreaves, as if he felt some sort of reaction to this was compulsory, said abruptly, 'We didn't know the full details ourselves until a day or two ago.'

Lambert regarded him quizzically for a long moment, whilst the man wished he had not spoken. Then the superintendent said, 'But you knew, one supposes, that your wife stood to inherit approximately a quarter of the total estate?'

'Er, yes. Yes, I suppose we did.'

Alison Hargreaves, as if irritated by her husband's air of evasion, said decisively, 'Every detail of my father's will was made clear to us approximately two years before his death, Superintendent. We didn't know the exact sum I would inherit, but if you are suggesting that the sum was large enough to provide us with a motive for wishing Dad out of the way, you are clearly right. But, as we have told you, neither of us was anywhere near High Beeches at the time when he was killed.'

'Quite. Well, as you know all the details of the will, you are plainly aware that there are several other people who will benefit substantially by your father's death. I have to ask you now if you have any thoughts on who might have killed him.'

She was a cool customer, this dark-haired, watchful, woman; her dark, almost black eyes were as bright and alert as a bird's. They dominated the calm face, giving the impression of taking in a wider spectrum than normal human eyes. He had no compunction about asking her whether she thought one of the family was involved in her father's murder.

She said, 'We've thought about that, of course. It's only natural that we should. I'm sure neither of my brothers was involved.'

It wasn't quite a full answer to his question, but he decided to take up the thought. 'How close were you and your brothers to your father, Mrs Hargreaves?'

For a moment she seemed about to treat this as an impertinence, as it would have been in anything other than a murder enquiry. Then she sighed and looked sideways at her husband, for the first time for several minutes. Again her eyes seemed bird-like, so that she was able to take a swift look at him with scarcely a movement of her head. 'Dad could be a difficult man to deal with. He was very stubborn at times. He became more so, I think, after my mother died. She was a restraining influence on him, with other people as well as with us.'

'He was a man who liked his own way?'

'Very much so.' Jim Hargreaves came in suddenly, as though anxious to support his wife, and then looked slightly embarrassed by his temerity. He felt uncomfortable now in his formal suit; it was preventing him from softening the interview into the friendlier exchanges he had envisaged.

Jim said in a more muted, apologetic tone, 'The trouble was that Mr Fletcher could be a hard man to cross. He didn't take criticism well.'

Hargreaves looked from his wife to the officers, as if hoping one party at least would give him encouragement to continue. His thin face held an almost desperate appeal beneath the thinning hair, his brown eyes widening like those of an anxious dog.

Lambert found himself wondering how this unassertive figure managed a class of secondary-school children. But as Christine reminded him when he spoke of such things, you could never predict success and failure in education; some teachers took on a different personality when confronted with a class of pupils or students.

It was Alison Hargreaves who now said, 'You've probably already heard that we had a bit of a family row two days before Dad died. If you haven't, you soon will.'

'We had heard. I gather you thought it would be advisable for him to enter a retirement home.'

'We put that suggestion to him, yes. Well, sheltered accommodation, actually, where he could have had his own flat. But the idea was not well received. In fact, he flew off the handle. But we should all have expected that.' This time she turned her head to look directly at her husband. He received a short but baleful look from those glittering dark eyes.

Lambert said, 'Forgive me for intruding upon family matters, but you will appreciate that in the circumstances it is inevitable. From all accounts, your father was in excellent health. If you thought that he would resist the idea of leaving his house, as you at any rate seem to have done, why did you put the idea to him? He seems to have been vigorous and determined, from your own account. The house shows no sign of neglect. And he had the admirable Mrs Brownrigg to help him and keep an eye on him.'

This time she was more than irritated: he was quite sure that she was furious. But she controlled her voice-level with difficulty, and said through tensed lips, 'Have you been talking to Brenda Collins?'

So there was animosity towards the woman – from the rest of the family as well, probably, but certainly from this vigorous and animated daughter of the dead man. Lambert said, in what might have been a parody of her even tone, 'Not yet. But we shall certainly be doing so in the near future.'

Alison Hargreaves smiled a mirthless smile. 'She will no doubt tell you that we were all after Dad's money. Well, it's right too, in a way. We felt that Dad would want to help us with our various plans, once he saw his money draining away into the fees for a home every week. He was a great one for making his money work for him, was Dad.'

For the first time there was real bitterness in her voice. Lambert felt his heart lift at the note. Murder turned things on their heads at times, for detectives as well as suspects. So Walter Fletcher hadn't been a benign old man with no enemies. He had been disliked, even hated, perhaps, by his own children, or one of them at least. When a victim has enemies, the hunt for his killer begins to offer up its scents.

He said carefully, 'In effect, some of your father's inheritors thought that they might get their hands on their inheritance a little earlier if he moved out of High Beeches?'

It was crude and direct, but intentionally so. Anger could make people more vulnerable and revealing of themselves than almost any other emotion. And his tactic only just failed to work.

The two faces opposite him lifted sharply. Jim Hargreaves at least would certainly have said something unguarded. But his wife's hand lifted six inches from her lap towards him, as she controlled herself with an effort she did not try to conceal. It was a moment before she said breathily, 'I suppose that would indeed be a fair summary of the strategy involved in persuading Dad to move out. Yes. It's a harsh way of looking at it, but I suppose an outsider would see it like that.'

Lambert forbore to ask what other way there might be of looking at the situation. Instead, he said, still prepared to needle them, 'I gather that, not surprisingly, your father did not take kindly to the idea. Presumably he realized that you were not primarily concerned with his welfare.'

'We weren't just being greedy. Dad would have been well looked after. He was getting less capable of looking after himself with each passing year.'

There should have been some regret, some sympathy, even perhaps some love, in such a statement for it to carry conviction. Alison Hargreaves made it a firm and businesslike assertion, no more.

But Lambert knew he had already carried this nearer to the point of outright rudeness than the unwritten codes of questioning permitted him. He said, including both of them in his question, 'Would you care to tell me what use of your father's money you had in mind for yourselves?'

For the first time, Alison Hargreaves held back, looking directly at her husband with those compelling eyes, inviting him to speak for them.

Jim Hargreaves had the grace to look embarrassed. He began rather indistinctly, then became clearer as his enthusiasm came through. 'I've always had the idea of starting my own school. There's room for one. Not in the Forest, but somewhere between here and Gloucester. Suitable places come on the market from time to time, and property prices are still depressed round here. Especially the larger properties that would be satisfactory for the establishment of a private school.'

In his discomfiture, he was talking too much. From what Christine had told him, Lambert doubted very much whether this was the moment to venture into private education. But he had no wish to get involved in that argument. He said to Alison, 'And your plan was to support your husband in this venture?'

She nodded, looking him straight in the face, defying him to challenge her. He wondered what this shrewd and dynamic woman thought of putting her share of her father's money into a private school. She did not look very enthusiastic. But her face might have been cut in stone; he was going to get nothing more from her.

He made a last attempt to dig in other areas. 'No doubt your brothers also had their plans, Mrs Hargreaves.'

'No doubt. You had much better ask them about that. I am quite sure you will be doing so.' She reached out well-manicured hands to take their cups, plainly signifying that she thought it was time to end this interrogation.

She was tight-lipped now. And Jim Hargreaves was nodding, taking his cue from her. Lambert said, 'We shall be seeing your brothers very soon, as you would expect. It will almost certainly be necessary for us to see you again, as the investigation develops and we are able to assemble more significant facts. Please do not go out of the area without leaving the details of your whereabouts at the police station in Oldford.'

The two detectives rose, surprisingly tall in the low-ceilinged modern room. They departed with the briefest of formal leave-takings, and the two people were left uncertain about the impressions they had created.

The Hargreaves stood by the wide modern window of their lounge, watching the CID men as they levered themselves stiffly into the old car and put on their seat belts. Neither of them spoke until the Vauxhall had disappeared towards the centre of the village.

Even then, Jim Hargreaves did not look at his wife as he spoke, but continued to stare after the vanished car. 'That sweater they took away,' he said. 'You didn't get that on the day your father died. You've had it for two months or more.'

10

One of the secrets was to dress well. The youth had decided that a year and more ago, when he had seen others busted whilst he went on his way unchallenged.

Well-dressed, of course, within the context of your group. You wore jeans and a T-shirt or a sweatshirt, depending on the weather. But you made sure that they were clean and fresh, even if they were well-worn. And in his case, you wore a clean example of the loose-fitting sweaters that were now blessedly fashionable. The sweater concealed the fact that you had sewn pockets on to the shirt beneath. Pockets for the materials in which you dealt.

For the youth accepted now that he was a professional trader. He sold things on a regular basis, like any other retailer. He acquired his goods as cheaply as he could, and sold them for the highest price he could command. Market forces, they called it. And this market was the most rapidly expanding one in the world.

The fact that it was an illegal one was unfortunate. But only in some ways: he found he regretted its unauthorized status much less than he had done when he began to deal. The risks were a little higher, but not unacceptable if you were shrewd and experienced. And there was no doubt that it was the illicit nature of the trade that was the basis of its high profits.

The youth strolled past the big Birmingham pub, with its bright lights and its neon invitations to happy hours and dancing. Jamaican rhythms pumped softly through the sound systems of its disco area. Those sounds would get louder as the evening advanced; he checked on his watch that it was still only twenty to nine.

He was not tempted to go into the place. There would be people looking for drugs in there, for certain, especially as the place got crowded in the last two hours of the day. But the police knew that as well as anyone; it was a place for amateurs, not professionals in the game like him. Most of it would be pot or temazepam, anyway, changing hands for a few pounds. No real money in those things for an ambitious entrepreneur.

The successful people in this game kept a lower profile, avoiding garish pubs like this. The pub where he had set up the deal was a quieter place, with no music. And with a quieter, more discerning clientele.

He walked on another half mile, to his chosen selling ground, savouring the keen night air of autumn, glad whilst he walked between the high buildings of the thick woollen sweater which would eventually be too warm in the pub. He was pleased to find that he was not at all anxious. It was hours now since his last fix, but the euphoria had not worn off yet. Just diminished to a feeling of healthy wellbeing, a confidence that he could handle himself and his trade. A good consignment, this coke. He would be able to vouch for that with a clear conscience when it came to selling it.

The soft lights behind the pub's Edwardian facade seemed to invite him through the darkness when he turned the corner, at once cheerful and discreet. This was an altogether more appropriate setting than the raucous den he had passed a little earlier for his biggest deal to date.

His contact was there when he got into the inn, sitting with a half-finished pint in front of him. He had a four-day growth of beard and a grey plaster on a damaged finger; a crescent of grimy skin poked through a frayed tear in the knee of his filthy jeans. His trainers had smears of oil and green across their once-white uppers, so that the youth's own new white Nikes looked almost unnaturally bright as he joined the man at the round table with its fretwork of cast iron beneath it.

He was irritated by the man's appearance. He was almost a caricature of the habitual user. His short hair at least was clean, but it was scarcely more than skinhead length: just the type to arouse police attention. He wondered whether to tell him about it. He thought he would, in a little while.

The man was probably three or four years older than him; twenty-four or -five, he would have guessed. It would give him a kick to issue directions to someone so much older and stronger than himself. And the man wouldn't argue, he'd be too anxious to obtain his coke and crack; he'd asked for both of them. He looked desperate already.

It gave one a feeling of power, as well as a good living, this trade. The youth liked that.

He bought the man another pint and himself a half of lager. He did not feel the need for a drink at all, really. When he'd been on ecstasy, he'd once become dehydrated, to the extent that no amount of liquid could satisfy his thirst. Nowadays, he only supplied that drug to others. Tonight, the fact that he felt no need for drink added to his feeling of power. But he sipped his half of lager, nevertheless. Professionals knew they must not make themselves conspicuous.

The youth went to the Gents in due course, checking that the floor was clean, that there were no telltale twists of tinfoil wrappings, as he was sure there would have been in that other pub he had passed nearer to the centre of the city. The place was clean, empty and smelling only of disinfectant. He chose the cubicle he would use if his purchasers preferred the melodrama of a secret exchange, then went back into the warmth of the pub.

It should be perfectly possible to conduct his transactions in the warm bustle of the public bar. This pub still had the mahogany and brass divisions of its Edwardian heyday. It had had a poor landlord and a low turnover in the seventies, when such furnishings had been ripped out of most other pubs in the chain. Now, ironically, both these fittings and the area where the inn was located had become fashionable again, as they had not been since the days before the First World War.

The design meant that a spacious bar area was divided into a series of more intimate squares that were almost separate rooms, except that they were open on one side for access to the bar. The youth liked this arrangement. If you were careful, you could conduct transactions in these settings as discreetly and less sordidly than in pub lavatories. It made him feel more like a businessman than a criminal.

Perhaps all this would become legal in due course. Already, the police turned a blind eye to cannabis users, though you had to be a bit more careful if you were dealing. And there were those who said that tobacco was more dangerous even than cocaine and heroin. Perhaps in thirty years all this would be legitimate – and thus much less profitable. But he would have made his pile by then, and be long departed into other tradings.

When he was not high on coke, when he had his periodic bouts of despair, he acknowledged that it was his own addiction that drove him to deal, so that he could be assured of the sums he needed to fuel his own intake. But with what his supplier had promised him, there would be enough now for more than that. With his new supplier, he was on the way to affluence; there was no doubt about that.

His customer was in no hurry to complete the deal, but the youth knew it would be all right. They had exchanged their coded signals when he arrived, and the scruffy man on the other side of the table knew that he had both the coke and the crack. He had been quite anxious to know about the price of the rocks, but he was quiet now.

The man's narrowed eyes flicked quickly from side to side over his pint glass. He stroked his stubbled chin as if it itched a little; after a short while, he went to the bar and bought the youth another half.

At this point, another man arrived, whom the scruffy one had vouched for. The youth saw a wad of notes when the newcomer went to the bar. Fifties, they were, there must be nearly a grand in his wallet. Then a girl came to join them, one he had met before. She was good-looking, in an angular sort of way, and cleaner than the other two.

He decided that the girl was also younger than the other two: about his own age, he thought. She became quite friendly with him; perhaps she realized that he could supply the quantities they wanted. He was quite clever, he thought, in suggesting that he might be able to do just that, without putting it into so many words.

If he and the girl met up again, as he hoped they would arrange to do at the end of the evening, he would try to get hold of some ecstasy. Made girls want sex, they all said, ecstasy did. Tactile, that was the word – he could not get it out of his mind. Well, he fancied being tactile himself. He imagined himself in bed with this girl, stroking her flanks, effortlessly supplying her with the satisfaction she craved after taking the ecstasy.

They played darts as the pub filled up and the level of noise, of argument and laughter, rose around them. He studied the dart in his hand for a moment, admiring the steadiness of his fingers and their grasp on the ferrule of the implement, even at arm's length. 'Quite good arrows, these,' he said. 'For a pub, I mean.'

Presently, the girl put her handbag on the table and the first man passed him money beneath the table. 'Five hundred,' he said, in what was little more than a whisper. He was excited, almost breathless. It made the youth feel in control of the situation and immensely superior. But he took care not to show it. Good salesmen were never patronizing. He had read that somewhere.

He looked round the pub, or what little they could see of it from their alcove, but casually, not stealthily. There was no need to be surreptitious, when you were in control. No one was paying much attention to the little group of four young people around the small round table.

He reached hurriedly beneath his sweater, producing the two polythene-wrapped packages. He passed them across the table behind the girl's handbag, feeling his way into the scruffy man's grasp, smiling at the girl to show her how confident he was. Perhaps he might even offer to take her home, in a few minutes; but he was still not quite sure what her relationship was with the other two.

He wondered afterwards if it was the girl who diverted his attention from any warning signs there might have been. He was aware of nothing until the man's hand moved from his fingers to his wrist, tightening suddenly like a vice.

It was the second man who grasped his shoulder and said, 'Dermot Fletcher, I arrest you on a charge of supplying illegal drugs. You are not obliged to say anything, but you should be aware that anything you do say will be recorded and may be produced in evidence.'

The first man was on his feet before the caution was complete, smiling a smile that contained both triumph and content. He said only, 'Let's go, sunshine.'

Dermot felt his legs suddenly weak as the police officers walked him into the cool air of the car park. It was the girl who drove the car. She did not look at him once after they had revealed their identity.

After they had parcelled the cocaine and the crack into a large labelled polythene container at the station, they made him empty his pockets, took away his belt and his shoelaces, told him about his rights to a phone call and a brief. Both their actions and his own passed like those of characters in a dream.

It was only when the cell door had clanged shut behind him and the drug-squad officers were going away that he heard the girl speak at last. Her voice was harsher than he remembered it in the pub, but he recognized her laugh.

'Poor bastard!' she said. 'He didn't know what day of the week it was.'

11

The first rain in three weeks was falling as Superintendent Lambert and Detective Sergeant Hook drove into the Forest of Dean to visit Brenda Collins.

A grey day after so much calm autumn sunshine, when water was forming pools in every hollow of tarmac, when leaves lay sodden at the roadside, when the Forest sheep peered resentfully at them through fringes beaded with moisture. Every house, every tree, every green rise of pasture seemed imbued with the prevailing dampness, as if the area welcomed this more normal end-of-October weather and sank happily into a sodden tranquillity. More than ever, this seemed an area which was designed to treat visitors as enemies, so that its denizens might deal with their own problems in their own way.

Lambert, sitting low in the passenger seat with his thoughts, felt a sullen indifference all around him, as the rain ran in rivulets down the windows and the car moved like a self-sufficient module through an alien world. The windscreen wipers moved in a rhythm that was almost hypnotic, the heat poured steadily into the car, the wheels swished through the surface water on the roads – and the doors remained resolutely closed on every house they passed. One would not have expected to see many folk abroad on a day like this, yet the absence of any visible human presence reinforced the impression that the Forest had made its preparations for their return by turning resolutely away from them.

And yet, despite the day and the environment, Lambert

felt a lifting of his spirits as they went. He had no idea yet who had done this murder, but he felt perversely that they were on the way to a solution. He would have scorned the word intuition, as a good professional should, but in truth there was nothing much more tangible to support his buoyant mood as yet.

They had still no guarantee that the culprit would emerge from the limited group of suspects on whom they were concentrating. Yet Lambert was more than ever convinced that this killer was among the family and close friends of the victim, among the seven people named in the will which old Arkwright had revealed to them so ponderously.

And the dead man had emerged now more clearly. Emerged not as the white-haired victim without vice which he had seemed when Hannah Hargreaves came to them with her suspicions about her grandfather's death, but as an altogether more wilful and cantankerous figure. A man who had made enemies, even amongst his intimates. A much more satisfactory victim, for a detective.

Resentments grew into hatreds, and hatreds gave motives. There was nothing more difficult to solve than a motiveless murder. There were passions here, among these people the investigation was still in the process of defining. And Walter Fletcher's death had precipitated the division of a surprisingly large estate. Where there was money, there were always the possibilities of villainy. You did not have to be a cynic to divine that: every criminal statistic supported the view.

The hunt was in full cry. As he advanced towards the quarry, the master of the CID hounds watched the rain fall and licked his lips in anticipation.

Brenda Collins was a surprise, even to men who had disciplined themselves to be surprised by nothing.

Those who had spoken of her had given the impression of a predatory female, of an opportunist who watched her chance to pounce upon and exploit an old man's

92

foolishness. Yet they found a woman who, in appearance at least, was as solidly reassuring as the mellow orange stone of her cottage.

Lambert stopped for a moment at the gate to appreciate the rich autumn colours of the collection of maples to his right, which seemed to blaze with a fresh defiance against the grey of the sodden sky behind them. Hook was more taken with the broccoli and sprouts of the neat vegetable garden to the side and rear of the building.

'More than I can eat myself. But I enjoy growing them, you see. And I freeze quite a lot.' She had managed to surprise them, appearing silently behind them from the other side of the building.

Brenda Collins was a cheerful, round-faced figure, with a plumpness which never approached obesity but seemed merely a reflection of health. She would have passed for much younger than sixty-eight, though she wore no make-up. She studied them with curious brown eyes and seemed not at all nervous. It was as though they and not she were to be investigated in this meeting.

The impression was reinforced when she took them into the comfortable interior of the cottage and sat them down in an armchair on each side of a red log fire, positioning herself between them and opposite the fire, as if anxious to give the best attention to both of her guests. She brought in a pot of tea and new-baked scones: already the cold grey dampness of the day had been excluded, and it seemed odd that they should ever have thought of this village as resentful of their presence.

Mrs Collins pushed two pieces of scone on to the plate of a willing Bert Hook. Putting his tea down upon the small table she had set at his elbow, she said, 'Walter always made for that chair when he came in here.'

So it was she who introduced, without embarrassment, the reason for their presence. Lambert, illogically irritated by this cosseting, said firmly, 'Mrs Collins, you will be aware that we are engaged in a murder investigation. In those circumstances, the police have access to any will left by the victim.'

She looked from one to the other of her visitors, a wide smile on the round face, removing most of the wrinkles which age had added over the years. 'You're talking about Walter's legacy to me? Bless him, he'd no need, but he wanted to do it, he said.'

'Twenty thousand pounds. A sizeable sum. You knew about that bequest before Mr Fletcher's death?'

If she knew that her answer would give her an immediate motive, she gave no sign of it. 'Yes. At least, I didn't know the exact sum, but he told me I'd been remembered. I didn't think about it much. He seemed set for a good many years yet. I thought I might be gone before him. He was only five years older than me, you know.' Her face was suddenly grave with the thought of mortality.

Bert Hook said, 'Have you any plans for the money?'

She looked at him, head a little to one side, deciding not to be insulted by the directness of his question, coming at her unexpectedly from this comfortable figure with the weatherbeaten face. She realized as clearly as he did that if she had plans for her legacy, it heightened the likelihood that she might have killed for it. She glanced at the table under the window, where a brochure with pictures of mountains and sea contrasted with the scene beyond the streaming glass.

Then she said, 'I'm using some of the money to go out to New Zealand in February, to see my daughter, Alice. But I could have done that without Walter's money. I've been saying I'd go for years, without getting round to doing it.'

'But the legacy will make it a little easier.' Hook was persuasive, but low-key. He did not look at her as he made the suggestion, but bit appreciatively into his second piece of scone.

They were a good pair, these two, she reckoned. They would have the truth of this out in the open before long, unless people were very careful. She said sadly, 'It will,

94

but that's not the reason why I've finally taken the plunge and booked. It's just that Walter was trying to persuade me to go on the last morning he was here.'

The cheerful round face with its neat frame of grey-white hair was suddenly sad with the memory. If she was acting this, she was doing it well. Lambert said, 'That was on the day before he died. Anything you can remember about your conversation that day could be important.'

She nodded. 'There'd been a bit of a row in the family, on the previous day. That's why Walter came here that morning, I think. I expect you've heard about it.'

'A little. We haven't heard much about Mr Fletcher's reaction to the quarrel. You can probably help us with that.'

At least they seemed to be presuming that she wanted to help them to catch Walter's killer. That must be a good thing, she imagined. She was surprised to find herself so cool in a situation that was so new to her. 'They suggested he might like to consider giving up his own house and going into sheltered accommodation.' She stopped and thought for a minute. 'At least, that's what he presumed it to be. It might just have been one of these apartments for retired people. I suspect Walter was too annoyed to find out the full details.' She smiled sadly, picturing his reaction when the idea was broached to him by his children.

Lambert cut into the thought. 'How well did Mr Fletcher get on with his family, Mrs Collins?'

She took her time, trying to frame her ideas so that they would be fair to the children and grandchildren as well as the man she had known for over sixty years. 'He wasn't always the easiest father to talk to, wasn't Walter. A bit suspicious of his children's motives, even when they were perfectly innocent. He got worse after his wife died. But you do, you know, when you're left on your own. You brood about things, if you're not careful.'

'So he was a difficult man to get on with?'

She thought for a moment, her face clouding a little

with sadness. Then she looked up, meeting the watchful eyes that were so coolly assessing her. 'He was a lovely man, was Walter. As far as I am concerned. But stubborn with his children. He used to say he was allowed to be bloody-minded, because they'd find he'd looked after them in the end. Well, he did, didn't he?'

She jutted the small round chin at them defiantly. Lambert said coolly, 'But he was made to look after them a little earlier than he meant to, Mrs Collins. Otherwise we wouldn't be here. And I'm sure you want us to find out who killed him.'

'Of course I do.' For the first time, she was a little ruffled, as he had intended. But she had control of her voice in an instant. 'I just pray that none of his family has done this, that's all.'

Lambert decided that she would be more likely to be frank about that family if he could stir up a little animosity in her. 'How do you think Mr Fletcher's children regarded his relationship with you, Mrs Collins?'

'What have they said?' The question was rapped at him, the single syllables like stones. The relaxed, almost jolly woman who had handled them with such aplomb was suddenly a termagant. But for a moment only. The effort to relax herself was apparent and undisguised, but it succeeded. The fingers which had clasped the arms of her chair so tightly straightened, then intertwined slowly with each other in her lap. She forced a smile as she said, 'But you wouldn't tell me what they said about me, would you?'

'Couldn't rather than wouldn't, Mrs Collins. We respect other people's confidences wherever we can. Just as we shall respect whatever you are going to tell us now about Mr Fletcher's family.'

Lambert was irritated and scarcely troubled to conceal it. He was being out-thought by a sixty-eight-year-old widow with no previous experience of police interrogation. She was composed again, when he thought he had disturbed her; a subject who was annoyed and defensive was far more likely to make unguarded statements than someone in full control. He said, 'Which of Mr Fletcher's children had thought up the plan to move him out of High Beeches?'

The broad brow furrowed, but he was not sure now whether it was a genuine attempt at recall or a mere simulation of it. 'I couldn't be sure of that. I don't think Walter knew that himself. If he did, he didn't relay the information to me.' Perhaps she saw annoyance flooding into his long, experienced face, for she added almost mischievously, 'I could speculate, of course, but that's all it would be.'

For a moment he almost bridled. Then he forced a smile and said stiffly, 'Informed speculation is always of interest at this stage of an investigation.' The very formality of his phrasing seemed defensive, an admission that she was conducting the interview on the lines she approved.

If she was aware of a contest between the two of them, she gave no sign. She was thinking hard about her next words. 'There's no doubt that all the children wanted to get their hands on some of Walter's money. I'm sure they hoped that when he was out of the house and with the money from its sale in his hands, he would be helpful with their various schemes. They were probably right in that. He was generous, when he thought it justified, was Walter. And he loved his children, though he wasn't always very good at showing it.'

'Why did they want money?' He left it as a bald question. He would like to have asked which of the offspring was most desperate for funds, but she might shy away from the suggestion, and she had already indicated that she would reveal information only on her own terms.

She looked from one to the other of the large men in front of her, as if persuading herself that the circumstances warranted her revelations of the secrets of her old friend. 'Alan is perpetually in need of funds. He works very hard in his nursery, and seems to be quite successful. But his ex-wife bleeds him of the profits, so that he seems always to be working hard to stand still. He needs to invest in new machinery and more glass to keep up with the opposition. He never says much, but I think he needs money pretty urgently.'

'Does he live and work on his own?'

She looked at him with those shrewd brown eyes, weighing his question and its implications. 'You mean is there another woman around. I don't think so. No, I'm sure there isn't. Not a serious long-term replacement for his wife. He seems too bitter for that – but you'll be able to size that up for yourselves when you see him.'

Lambert noted that she knew that they hadn't yet interviewed Alan Fletcher; no doubt she knew just as clearly that they had already seen his sister and her husband. The village grapevine, relaying the news of the interlopers' activities, was as efficient as he had known it would be. And now this cool woman was taking full advantage of her knowledge. He said querulously, 'I wanted to know also whether Alan Fletcher has any paid help at the nursery.'

'No. He could do with it, but he can't afford it. He has a woman in to help him prepare the produce for market for a few hours at the height of the season, but that's all.' She hesitated, then decided that, as they would come to this anyway, she would take the initiative herself. 'Alan would like to have employed his son, Dermot, and passed the nursery on as a going concern to him in due course. But with what he has to take out for his wife, it would never support the two of them. He had the idea that if he could develop the business, it would be the salvation of his son.'

'And was that idea realistic? Would the prodigal son have come home and worked every day growing vegetables and fruit?'

She shrugged. 'Perhaps not. I don't know either Alan or his son well enough to offer an opinion to you on that. But the essential thing surely is that Alan thought he could bring Dermot back and solve his problems if he had more capital to develop the place.'

It was true, of course. But that made it no more pleasant that he should be reminded of it by this clear-sighted pensioner. He said hastily, brutally, 'Do you think Dermot could have killed his grandfather?'

'No. But then, I can't conceive how any of the family would have killed Walter. Dermot is as likely as anyone. He was around here at the time.'

'You saw him on the day of the murder?' Lambert wondered if the words came from him too eagerly.

'No. But Bella was around.' She saw their puzzlement. Any villager would have known immediately what she meant. She said with a touch of impatience, 'Bella's a black Labrador. Dermot's dog. Or, strictly speaking, Alan's dog. But from the moment she arrived, when Dermot was only about thirteen, the two of them have been inseparable. Even now that Dermot's away so much, the two of them are together from the moment when he gets home.'

Canine loyalty is unshaken by drug convictions and other human transgressions, thought Lambert. Its simple, unswerving intensity is one of its greatest attractions. But the bond, like all forms of love, can be a weakness to those with things to conceal. 'You saw the dog on the day Mr Fletcher was killed?'

'No. I saw her on the day before Walter died, in the lane outside here. I remember thinking then that Dermot must be home. He takes her for walks, you see. I don't think Alan ever does that – he's much too busy. The dog has to exercise itself by following him about the nursery.'

Yet they had already been told that a dog had been seen near High Beeches on the day of the murder . . . But for all they knew Brenda Collins could be deliberately planting this idea, for reasons of her own. Lambert said, 'What about Mr Fletcher's other son?'

'Chris is a quiet man. The scholar of the family. Too mild and quiet to be a murderer.' She waited a moment for a reaction. When none came, she said, 'But people said that about Crippen, I expect.' The brittleness of her laughter was the first revelation that this was an ordeal for her, however effectively she had disguised the fact.

'Was Christopher Fletcher short of money?'

'Yes. I'm sure he was. He doesn't have expensive tastes, and he has only himself to support, but I'm sure that bookshop of his has never paid a living wage. If he didn't live so modestly, he'd have had to give it up years ago.' She didn't say 'and do some proper work' but her sturdy countrywoman's assessment of the situation implied the thought.

That made the fact that Christopher Fletcher had enquired about the lease of another bookshop a month before his father's death all the more interesting. But there was no reason to reveal the results of the preliminary CID enquiries to this well-organized woman. Not at this stage.

Lambert watched Hook writing industriously in his notebook for a moment, then said, 'What about Mr Fletcher's daughter, Alison?'

'They wanted money for something, she and Jim. I don't know what. Walter didn't know himself, though Alison had told him that they needed money.'

So Brenda Collins didn't know about the private school project that Jim Hargreaves was nurturing. Or she said she didn't: investigators always had to add that irritating rider to any answer, until they were convinced that the person involved had no connection with the crime. Lambert said, 'Did Alison appear desperate for funds?'

Brenda Collins thought for a moment. If there was any animosity between her and Walter Fletcher's daughter, it wasn't revealed in her attitude. 'I don't know. Walter was surprised that she lent herself so readily to the plan to move him out of his house. But she could have genuinely thought it was a good idea. For Walter, I mean. There were things in its favour, you know. It isn't always a lot of fun, living on your own.' She looked her age for the first time, as a mixture of tiredness and sadness stole into her face.

Lambert knew that this was the nearest thing to a right moment for the question he had to ask. 'Mrs Collins, you are too intelligent a woman not to appreciate that your relationship with Walter Fletcher was bound to be a subject of interest and conjecture.'

'You mean the family were scared he might marry me?' The swiftness and directness of her reply sounded like a rebuke to his prolixity. She grinned in fond recollection. 'Walter liked to set them thinking about that. Let them see there was life in the old dog yet, he said. But if you really want to know, we had no intention of marrying. Both of us had been very close to our spouses – I can't get used to calling them partners. Walter and I were good friends, and we confided in each other. Walter was content as he was, and so was I.' She looked at him impishly, and Lambert could see the young girl who had turned heads half a century ago. 'You men aren't always as desirable to have about the house as you think, you know.'

And thus the interview came to an end. They had covered the ground they planned, but it still felt at the end as though it was Brenda Collins who had concluded things and dismissed them.

Bert Hook had been up early for the television programme on his Open University literature course. As he drove carefully beneath leaden skies along the gloomy lanes, he kept his gaze firmly fixed on the next bend ahead and his lips rigidly still. It would never do to let a superintendent see a sergeant smiling at his discomfiture, especially when it came from an elderly woman with the looks of a Hardy peasant and the brain of a Jane Austen.

He need not have worried. Lambert's eyes were closed. He was wrestling with the thought that, whether or not Walter Fletcher had purposed to marry Brenda Collins, his family had thought he might. Which meant that any one of them might have moved swiftly, to forestall a marriage which might have deprived him or her of an inheritance.

12

Jim Hargreaves was glad the school day was over, as he usually was nowadays. He found children en masse more and more taxing. The diminishing noise of their shrill, departing voices from the school drive was one of the more consoling sounds in an exhausting life.

Automatically, he moved the untidy heap of exercise books his last charges had slung on to the table at the front of the classroom as they left into a neat pile. Then he switched off the overhead projector he had used during the last lesson and put away his transparencies. There was no doubt in his mind that he had earned a cup of tea.

The Forest of Dean Secondary School was less than fifteen years old. With falling rolls taking their toll on pupil numbers, it already held over a hundred fewer pupils than the nine hundred it had been built for. Jim should by now have had smaller classes and more opportunity to take account of the learners' individual needs.

Some hope! he thought, as he put away the big map of Europe he had been using. The market-forces economy of the nineties meant that classes had remained the same size, with redundancies among the teaching staff and the perpetual threat of unemployment brandished over those who argued against the system. Jim and his fellow teachers found themselves watching each other, storing their thoughts about their colleagues as ammunition for those commissioned to wield the axes of redundancy.

Or so it seemed to Jim Hargreaves. He was not among the most efficient of the staff, and the unspoken questions over his future in the school came as much from within himself as from any other quarter. He found that he did not mix with the rest of his colleagues in the staff room as eagerly or as easily as he had done a few years earlier.

He kept more and more to his Geography Room, like an embattled subaltern avoiding a Mess which no longer extended its sympathy. In the small storeroom which the architect had obligingly provided for him, he had a kettle, a table, and three rather uncomfortable stand chairs. All the walls were lined with shelves for the department's stock of textbooks and materials, and there was no window. The only illumination came from the harsh but efficient fluorescent tubes against the low ceiling.

Some would have found this a depressing place in which to spend much time. Jim Hargreaves found increasingly that it was the only place where he could relax.

He moved a box of the hard white chalk that he used less and less nowadays from the scratched table on to one of the shelves; modern chalk was supposed to be dustless, but traces of it found their way nevertheless into cups and kettle if you left it around. He poured the boiling water straight over the single teabag in the stained mug; Alison said you should always use a teapot, even for one, but he found that here he always brewed it straight into the cup. It took less energy, and he could hardly tell the difference in the taste.

By the time he had emptied the beaker, the school, or that part of it around the Geography Room, was silent. Jim felt very tired; sitting down with the tea seemed to have increased rather than relieved his fatigue. Suddenly, amidst his lassitude, he was seized by the conviction that he could not continue to live his life like this.

The children at school were getting more and more difficult for him to control. He was quite good with the sixth formers for A levels, but anyone who understood the job knew that they were the easiest groups to teach. Jim sounded off like the other staff about the modern lack of parental control and adolescent contempt for authority of any kind, but he was too intelligent not to realize that most of his problems came from within himself.

'A dutiful rather than a gifted teacher', the report had read after his first, probationary year in teaching. Now, all these years later, he felt the accuracy of that judgement weighing more heavily than ever upon his shoulders. He was never inspired with a class, never more than competent – and sometimes, when control became difficult with an unruly set, much less than that.

And where once he would have hurried home to his wife for consolation and support, he now sat alone with his tea in this warm little cell. He didn't know quite what had gone wrong between him and Alison. Perhaps his lethargy, which he carried home with him as he had not done in the early years, was the reason for the decline in the intensity of their love. It wasn't just sex – though he must face up soon to the fact that all wasn't as it should be there.

He must have it out with Alison. They could make a fresh start now, and it was up to him to see that they did. But she never seemed to want to talk, and he seemed to have lost not only the energy but the very will to make her discuss things. Strangely, things seemed to have got worse since Hannah went off to university. Now, when they should be closer to each other than ever in the empty house, Alison and he seemed to be getting further apart.

Well, he must find the will to change that. There was ample opportunity now, with the legacy coming to them. They would go to look at possible sites for the new school on Saturday morning. Alison had said sensibly enough that they mustn't appear too eager, but he knew that he couldn't let things go on like this.

The resolution cheered him a little. In a moment, he would gather together his books for marking, pack his briefcase, and drive home.

When he heard the door open beyond the walls of his storeroom, he thought at first that it was the caretaker coming into the classroom. But he recognized the voice which called out 'Jim?' immediately, so that he had donned a smile by the time the figure in the worn sports coat and suede shoes came into his retreat.

Simon Marsden was a little older than Jim. He must be almost fifty now, though usually he seemed rather less than that. He was a more successful teacher than Jim, popular with the children, with that knack effective teachers have of securing discipline simply by expecting it. He had joined the staff to teach English at the same time as Jim, and they had remained friends ever since they had met each other on that first day twelve years ago.

Like many educators, Marsden concealed a genuine idealism beneath a veneer of scepticism. He maintained a sardonic questioning of the latest educational jargon, of the motives of those faceless moguls who compelled the latest curriculum changes upon the practitioners at the chalk face, and it made him a popular member of the staff room.

But today his brow was uncharacteristically clouded as he came through the classroom and into the storeroom. He refused the offer of tea and stood looking down at his friend, ignoring the chair which Jim had pushed back for him.

'There's something I wanted to sort out,' he said.

And in that moment, Jim knew with a sinking heart what it was. He said, 'Sure. Did you want a baby-sitter over half-term or something?' Simon had four children, two of them still young.

'No. Nothing like that.'

'Well, what then?' Jim found himself licking his lips, even as he forced a smile. 'It isn't that you want me to –'

'No. It's that Tuesday afternoon, a fortnight ago. When you asked me to say you were in the staff room for those two free periods you had.'

Jim affected to be puzzled, but it was not an effective pretence. He managed a shrug of his shoulders, but he heard his own voice quaver as he said, 'I don't quite remember –'

'You should have told me at first what it was all about. I thought I was just covering you for a trip into town to buy a birthday present for Alison. If you'd only –'

'All right, my fault. It doesn't matter.'

Hargreaves spoke the words in such a hopeless monotone that his friend looked sharply down at the pinched white face beneath the thinning hair, then lowered himself on to the stand chair he had previously refused. 'I'm sorry, Jim. But you didn't explain at the time what was involved. I don't want to let you down, really I don't, but I don't see how . . .'

His voice tailed off, and the desperate man beside him saw in the hesitation, in the softening of his attitude, a gleam of hope. 'It's important to me, Simon. More important than you know. If you could just –'

'But I do know, Jim, now. You're involved in a murder investigation. You're using me as your cover for that afternoon.'

Hargreaves sighed. Preoccupied with his own problems, he had not thought that the connection with his father-in-law's death would be made so readily in the school. He said, 'Yes, I am using you. Perhaps I shouldn't be. Perhaps as you say I should have told you what was involved for me from the beginning. But you must see now how important it is for me that –'

'You still don't see, do you, Jim?' It was the first time that Marsden had raised his voice. His eyes widened with the attempt to convince this stubborn man who would not see things for what they were. 'You have to realize that it's the very seriousness of what's involved that means I can't hold my tongue about it. It would make me an accessory after the fact, or whatever they call it.'

He's presuming I'm guilty already, thought Jim. And this is my friend. He raised the beaker to his lips, only to find that it was cold and empty. He said dully, 'If that's how you feel, there's nothing I can do about it.' His brown

106

eyes stared unseeingly at the scratched and dusty table.

Simon was suddenly very sorry for the defeated figure beside him. He said, 'Look, I don't want to get you into any trouble. I'm not going looking for people to tell them that you weren't in the school on that Tuesday afternoon. But if the police come and ask me, I'll have to tell them, that's all I'm saying.'

Jim Hargreaves made the best he could of it. 'All right. That's all I was expecting, really. I don't suppose anyone will actually question you about it.'

Simon Marsden left quickly then, before their friendship could be strained any further. He had produced that 'accessory after the fact' phrase without thinking about its implications. It was only when his old car had moved beyond the school gates and into the gathering darkness that the thought came to him that he might actually be shielding a murderer.

Detective Inspector Christopher Rushton was prepared for opposition when he went up to Birmingham to interview Dermot Fletcher.

The Drugs Squad preferred to keep their captures to themselves. That was understandable, for they were engaged in a war, where individual prisoners were often interesting only as a means of access to the commanders behind them. Dermot Fletcher had already been charged with drug-dealing, so that they could keep him in captivity. But his case was of little interest to the drugs officers, though his conviction would be straightforward enough in due course. It was as a possible conduit to darker and vaguer figures in the Stygian darkness of the drug underworld behind him that he was of use to the Drugs Squad.

They guarded Dermot Fletcher jealously, and kept him isolated whilst they conducted a series of interrogations. The initial reaction to the call from Oldford CID was one of scarcely veiled hostility. But when the Oldford interest in the boy was explained, they conceded that they must allow access to Fletcher, reluctantly but without any real argument. Murder investigations instilled awe and overrode other protocol, even among the hard men who fought in the drugs war.

DI Rushton was given an interview room and a detective constable to support him. He was in no hurry to start the interview, waiting until Dermot Fletcher had been seated on the other side of the small square table for several seconds before he switched on the tape recorder and announced that the interview was beginning.

Fletcher was white and drawn. By this time, he was resigned rather than apprehensive. He had gone through too many interviews about his drugs connections to present anything but a weary confusion to this new challenge. If he had any idea what this was about, he gave no sign of it. He slumped abruptly on to the chair and stared incuriously at Rushton.

In twenty minutes, it would be time for the fix the law allowed him, as a confirmed addict. Already that thought was dominant in his exhausted mind, and Rushton knew it, just as clearly as he knew the limited time he had with the man.

'So you're in big trouble, lad.' The parchment face opposite him neither confirmed nor denied the notion. No doubt the seriousness of the drugs charges had been amplified to him at length over the preceding two days. 'And I'm here to make it bigger, I'm afraid.'

Still no sign of curiosity. Perhaps he had already endured too many police threats. Rushton said, 'We've been looking for you for days, Dermot. Then you obligingly walk into our hands because of the drugs.' It was true: he wouldn't tell him that the search had almost missed him because of the very fact that he was in custody on other charges.

The dark eyes, unnaturally large within their deep hollows, lifted briefly towards him with what might have been the first hint of curiosity. The grey lips scarcely

108

moved as Fletcher said wearily, 'What do you want with me now?'

Rushton, who prided himself on being a tough interrogator, felt a sudden shaft of pity piercing the disgust he had planned to sustain throughout the interview. This lad, whom the charge-sheet said was twenty-one but who looked like an ailing thirty-year-old, was alone like him, alone on an infinitely harsher battlefield.

When Rushton had finished here, he would go back to an empty house, sterile of affection as the barest cell since the departure of his wife and child. He would have only his own company to fill the quiet rooms, and recently he had found that to be the most unwelcome fellowship of all. But this man would go back to a real cell, senses dulled by the poison he needed now as medicine. He would await trial and sentence, then serve his time, two or three to a cell, with men who would find his youth an incitement to buggery or sadism.

That was unless he was guilty of the most ancient and gravest of all crimes. Rushton said, 'I'm from the CID Division at Oldford. I'm here because we're investigating a murder.'

Fletcher twitched a little, then gave a tiny nod. They were his first real reactions, and Rushton was grateful to have a starting point. He said, 'The murder of your grandfather, Walter Fletcher.'

'I heard about Granddad. You're saying he was murdered?' There was no surprise in the question, only the slightest quickening of interest. Rushton was irritated, not so much by Fletcher as by the drugs to which the man had consigned his will and energies. They made it impossible to seek and find the reactions in him which might be significant. Was this really the first time that the youth had contemplated the fact that the old man might have been murdered, or was it a pathetic attempt at dissimulation?

'Your grandfather was deliberately and brutally killed by someone who knew quite clearly what he was about. Someone who tipped him off the top of his ladder and

109

left an old man bleeding to death from a fractured skull.'
Rushton threw in the harsh phrases, watching his subject
for a reaction.

The dark eyes stared at him, widening a little. Behind
their glazing, there stirred what might have been speculation. Then Dermot Fletcher gave a brittle laugh and said,
' "Who would have thought the old man to have had so
much blood in him?" eh?' For a moment he was as proud
as a schoolboy of this quotation. Then his eyes flashed
briefly to the ceiling, as if he recognized even through the
fog of his addiction that this was in bad taste.

Rushton searched through the memory section of his
own more tidy mind. This was Macbeth the boy was quoting. Or Lady Macbeth. That murder had been the result
of a combination. Was young Dermot suggesting there
might be a conspiracy in this murder? Or was he merely
prompted by the appalling recollection of the old man's
shattered corpse, as he had himself stood over it at the
foot of that ladder?

'Did you kill him, Dermot?'

'No. I haven't spoken to him for nearly three years. Not
since I took the money.'

Rushton felt the detective's thrill which came always
with the chance discovery of new knowledge. People often
supposed that the police machine was omniscient, and
that was a useful delusion to foster. The inspector, searching for a neutral phrase to disguise his ignorance, came
up with, 'Your grandfather took that badly?'

'Oh, yes. It was only twenty pounds, but I'd just picked
it up off his table when he was out of the room. I needed
it for some coke, you see.' He had the drug-user's lack of
moral sense, which made that seem explanation enough.
'Granddad ordered me not to go back to his house again.
He was quite right, of course. I was ashamed – I was still
capable of being ashamed then, of course.' The grey lips
framed a thin, mirthless smile at the memory of the youth
that was gone.

Rushton said stiffly, 'You'll be treated, you know, for

110

the drugs, whatever happens. It will be up to you to stay off them.' It was not part of his normal interviewing technique to offer such sympathy, but from the isolation of his own loneliness, he ached unexpectedly for the desolation of the hollow-eyed figure on the other side of the table.

Fletcher did not even look at him. He brought both his hands slowly on to the table in front of him, studying their trembling as if they were the hands of some other being. In a throaty voice, he said, 'I need a fix.'

'Soon, Dermot. Did you kill your grandfather?'

Fletcher did not look up, even at that. He shook his head, as if the hands before him were still his greater concern. His right arm gave a sudden twitch, and he looked for a moment like a surprised child.

Rushton glanced down at his wrist, at the watch the prisoner was not allowed. He had a maximum of five minutes left. 'Who did kill the old man, Dermot?'

'I don't know.'

'You must have your own ideas.'

A brief, violent shaking of the head. He was losing physical control of his movements. Rushton said, 'You were in the area at the time.' There was no reaction from the other side of the table. 'You were seen, you know. With your dog.'

He looked up at that, fear in his sunken eyes for the first time. But not for himself. 'Is Bella all right? It's not her fault, you know.'

He seemed to think the dog might be in danger from its very proximity to this killing. Did that mean that she had been there with him when the old man fell? 'Bella's all right, Dermot. She's at home with your dad. But where was she when your grandfather died?'

'I don't know. Bella hadn't anything to do with it.' He was showing more concern for the dog's imagined danger than for his own real one.

'She was there with you on the day before Walter Fletcher died. You were seen.'

This time there was the briefest of nods; the head moved as jerkily as a puppet's, giving the illusion that it might at any moment detach itself. Rushton did not trouble to make him confirm the admission vocally for the tape: in Fletcher's condition, this recording wasn't going to be worth a lot as evidence.

'Was Bella there with you again, on the afternoon when your grandfather was killed?'

'No. Not with me. I didn't do it.' The staccato phrases came automatically. They might be no more than a routine, instinctive denial. Then, with a last appeal, the youth half fell against the table. 'I don't know where I was on that afternoon. The days merge into each other.'

The time was up. Rushton said, not unkindly but without much hope of success, 'You'd better give it some thought, lad, when your brain is calmer. It's in your own interest to recall where you were on that afternoon.'

On the short journey back to his cell, they half carried the exhausted figure who might be a murderer.

13

Christopher Fletcher was trying not to get too excited about his legacy. Money had never meant much to him in the past, and he had been proud to demonstrate that. To his brother and sister, with their family responsibilities and consequent need for financial planning, he had sometimes seemed tiresomely unrealistic, even a little priggish.

Now, for the first time in his life, he found himself excited, not by the large sum of money which was coming to him, but by the possibilities it opened up in his life. He had already been down to the bank to announce that his overdraft was about to be cleared, and been received unctuously by a manager suddenly anxious to assist with the investment of his new fortune.

It was the first time in his life he had been made aware of the different status accorded by money. He found it a pleasantly disturbing experience. He was too intelligent not to smile wryly at his new status, but human enough to be excited by the range of choice now open to him.

Moreover, for the first time in his life, he was making choices with another person who was close to him. That was the strangest and most exciting sensation of all. And the police seemed to be accepting his story; no one had challenged him about the concealments it contained.

He played with a few figures on a single sheet of paper at the desk in his shop in Cinderford. On this drab morning of autumn dampness in the Forest towns, there was no trade to disturb him. It was only just after nine, but he had been at his desk for half an hour now; he had found himself too excited to sleep and had risen early.

But it was a happy excitement, and he had found it difficult at first to keep still, until he became absorbed in his new plans. The damp cold did not seem to be bringing the pain to his damaged leg, as it usually did. His sharp pencil raced rapidly over the paper, the figures of his calculations delicate and precise.

Chris drew a satisfied line under the total at the base of the sheet, then stared at the complete set of leatherbound Dickens which was to have a position of prominence in the new shop. He could see it now in his mind's eye: at the back of the window display, out of the sun, but picked out discreetly by the concealed lighting.

It was amazing how capital opened up possibilities he had never even been able to contemplate before in the world of book-selling. Even now, a fortnight after his father had died, he had to keep reminding himself that what he had always dreamed about was now going to be the reality.

He would have to learn how to use a computer when they were installed in the new shop, he supposed. And he must practise placing his orders by fax, as if he had been doing it for years. The anticipation was deliciously pleasurable, as well as a little frightening. But he hugged the most exciting idea of all to himself again: he would be entering this brave new world not alone, but with a cherished companion.

Presently, he made the phone call he had been intending throughout the morning. The voice he had longed to hear answered after two rings, as if it too had been waiting for the moment. Chris said, 'The solicitors say the probate business is quite straightforward. We should have the money within six weeks. So we can put a bid in for new premises any time from now onwards.'

It was delicious to hear the excited anticipation in that other voice. Chris listened to the enthusiasm answering his own with a steady smile, then gently vetoed the idea of a shop in Hay-on-Wye, the self-styled 'second-hand book capital of the world'.

'The town gets plenty of visitors, but it's crowded with people who just want to run a bookshop,' he said loftily. 'They're not worried about profits and turnover: it's unfair competition for a project like ours. We're going to make money, don't forget!'

It was good to be the lofty champion of commercialism and pragmatism to one who knew so much less than he did about the book business. He said, 'I've got the details of two possibilities from the agents. One is in Chepstow – you can see the edge of the castle from the front door – and the other one's near the abbey in Tewkesbury. Both of them have the bonus of tourist-buying to eke out the steady local trade. I'll bring the details over tonight and we'll have a look at them together. If we think it worthwhile, we'll run over and inspect one or both of them on Sunday.'

Even after he had put the phone down, the smile clung to Chris's ascetic features. He hoped he had not appeared too masterful in his knowledge of the trade. If the truth were told, he had been unworldly for years in his attitude to books and bookshops. But that was going to change, now that the new business would be supporting two of them.

Chris was still staring fondly at the phone when it chirruped sharply into life. He snatched it up with a lover's eagerness, his first thought being that the voice still nestling in his ears was back with some query or suggestion.

Instead, the message was businesslike, the tone professionally neutral. 'Mr Christopher Fletcher? This is Detective Sergeant Hook of Oldford CID. It's in connection with the investigation into the murder of your father. Superintendent Lambert and I need to see you. Later today . . . Yes, I know you have, but there are some supplementary questions deriving from the statement you gave to our officer which we need to clarify . . . No, we have already arranged to see your brother later this morning. We'll come to your shop early this afternoon.'

This time Chris did not smile at the instrument when he had put it slowly back into its cradle. He was overcome instead by a sudden apprehension.

Christine Lambert was spoiling her husband. Half-term had released her from school routine, and she had made John promise to go in a little later this morning. After all, he had not arrived home until almost ten on the previous evening.

As a reward, she had cooked him the bacon-and-egg breakfast which was so rare as to be almost an annual treat for him nowadays. He ate it slowly, with every appearance of enjoyment. Yet she knew him well enough after almost thirty years to recognize the abstraction in his face. After five years of their marriage, his inability to switch off from work when he came into the house had once almost split them up. That old war seemed to belong now to another world.

John Lambert found it easier now to let go, to avoid treating every case as some kind of personal feud. He made more time for his grandchildren, when they were around, than he ever had for his children. But when he was on a murder case, he still tended to forget everything else.

Christine said, 'If Keith is offered a job out there and they have a decision to make, we mustn't seem to be standing in their way.'

He looked up at her, his face so full of incomprehension that she wanted to laugh, despite her irritation. 'New Zealand, John. I told you all about it last night. Jacqueline called yesterday afternoon. There's a possibility that the firm may offer Keith promotion out there.'

John Lambert tried to drag back a brain that was reluctant to emerge from the Forest of Dean. 'Nice place to bring up a family,' was all he could manage.

'And on the other side of the world from their grandparents.'

'We could visit.'

'Oh, yes. Drag you away from your work and your garden and your golf, could I, during my summer holidays?'

He was going to say that it would be winter then, in New Zealand, but he sensed that the notion would not be well received. He said lamely, 'Well, it will probably never happen. No use getting excited, until we see how definite it's likely to be.'

She didn't want common sense from him: not with her daughter and the little ones moving to the other side of the world. She could feel them moving into one of their rows; not the old, fierce ones they used to have, when she was imprisoned in the house with two toddlers who scarcely saw their father, but one of the lower-key ones they had nowadays, which were never quite resolved. She wanted him to say how much he would miss his daughter and his grandchildren, even if they were going to a splendid place. Instead, he said, 'Do you keep the receipt, when you buy clothes at Marks and Spencer's?'

It was such an unexpected switch that she replied before she had time to be annoyed. 'Yes. Until I've tried the things on, at any rate. They make a big thing of their willingness to change things, you see.'

'So most people who had a cardigan still neatly folded in its wrapper would have the receipt with it?'

'Yes. Unless they'd tried it on and found they were satisfied with it, of course. But then they probably wouldn't put it carefully back into the packaging.'

She did not ask about the reasons for his interest, and he went off swiftly after a glance at the clock. They had never 'darlinged' each other, and he did not kiss her when he left in the mornings. But she knew he was preoccupied when he omitted even the ritual jokes about his fried breakfast.

She watched him crunching over the gravel to the old Vauxhall Senator which he still refused to change. He had thickened a little about the waist, but nothing like as much

117

as most of his contemporaries. His hair was plentiful still, but greying a little more each year; his tall man's stoop was slight, but noticeable in one who had once been so much a ramrod. He climbed stiffly into the driving seat of the big car, and she wanted suddenly to run to him, to put her arms round him protectively.

She did not do it, of course. They had grown up in an age when you were taught not to indulge in public displays. John Lambert drove carefully between the gateposts, with their scatterings of yellow leaves, and disappeared without looking back.

14

Alan Fletcher was as active that morning as his brother was reflective. Even though the previous week's adjustment to Greenwich Mean Time meant that the light crept into his east-facing bedroom an hour earlier now, he was up when dawn broke over the silent earth and glass of his smallholding. By six-thirty he was at work, and he laboured without any real pause for three hours. Even he could not have said for certain whether the physical labour was intended to keep his mind from dwelling on the impending visit from the CID.

They came exactly at the time they had arranged, the tall superintendent and the bulkier sergeant behind him, picking their way carefully over the old cobbles towards the long glasshouse, observing his methodical work for a moment before moving the sliding door and allowing Bella's single bark to alert him to their presence.

On this morning of clammy cold, he was warm from his efforts with spade and fork, but his visitors were glad of the heat from the old Aga in the big kitchen. They sat on the worn stand chairs at the scrubbed deal table, with Fletcher on one side and the two detectives observing him from across the bare wood. Almost like an interview room, thought Hook. Yet it was Alan Fletcher, not they, who had set up this framework for the exchange.

He washed his soil-encrusted hands briefly at the sink, glancing at the big round clock above him. Bella went and lowered herself cautiously to lie by the stove, watching

119

the scene at the table for a moment, then dropping her head on to her paws as her eyes gradually closed.

Alan said, 'This won't take long, will it? I have to get the last tomatoes of the season to the market; I've been lifting the plants this morning.' It was his first lie, and an unnecessary one: the tomatoes were to be collected. They were lying ready in the shed in their shallow boxes. He wondered why he had said it. Probably it was just because he wanted this over as quickly as possible.

Lambert's long face and cool grey eyes gave him the impression that his small untruth had been spotted immediately, though that was surely impossible. The superintendent said drily, 'We shall take as long as is necessary, Mr Fletcher. You would expect that in a murder enquiry.'

Alan looked at him for a moment, then nodded roughly. He said, 'Do you want a drink? Tea or coffee?' He had not realized until that moment how much he needed one himself. He had worked without pause for three hours, bending and lifting with fork and spade; moreover, he found as he sat stiff-backed at his own table that his lips had gone very dry.

'No, thank you. We shall keep you from your work as little as possible.' If Lambert realized that he had turned Fletcher's argument back upon him, there was no sign of it in his even tone. 'We have the statement that you gave to our officer. We should like to amplify it in some areas.'

Alan nodded. Presumably it was a copy of his statement that the stolid figure who had been introduced as Sergeant Hook was now looking at in his folder. For the tenth time since he had heard of this visit on the previous evening, Alan went over in his mind what he had said to the patient, unthreatening constable who had compiled this.

Then Lambert said abruptly, 'Tell us about this row you had with your father two days before he died.'

'It wasn't just me.' The words came out too vehemently, so that he found both of the men on the other side of the table looking at him speculatively. 'And I'm not sure you should call it a row. A family disagreement, you might say.

120

We wanted Dad to move out of High Beeches, that was all. He didn't want to, and he got annoyed. He shouldn't have done, because we'd never have made him go, but he had a short fuse when he got annoyed, did Dad.'

So far so good. He had delivered this exactly as he had planned it. It had come out rather like that, perhaps – too prepared – but they couldn't make anything of that.

'So the family had got together before that Sunday, and agreed to present a united front to the old man.'

'Yes.' It sounded bad when they put it like that, as if his father had not been the formidable, even fearsome, figure which all of them had found him. 'We thought we were acting for his own good as well, you know.'

'As well as what, Mr Fletcher?'

'Well, as well as for ourselves, I suppose.' Alan wondered whether to clam up on them, then realized that it was bound to come out, that they might even already know. 'We all needed money, for different reasons. Dad had sold a prosperous business. He also lived in a big house, which is worth a lot of money. We thought if he released his capital, he would be more prepared to help us than to see it lying in the bank.'

'And being eroded by nursing-home charges, no doubt.'

'Perhaps that, too. He certainly wouldn't have liked to see large sums of money dribbling away month by month, wouldn't our dad. He'd rather it had gone to us – done us some good. He cared about us, really.'

That was the real tragedy of this case, thought Lambert. That craggy old curmudgeon had cared about his family and his friends, beneath his crustiness. But it was one of them, in all probability, who had seen fit to dispatch him. He said, 'Who is "us" in this context, Mr Fletcher? The whole family, including grandchildren?'

Alan shook his head vigorously. 'No. The three of us. Chris and Alison and me.'

'But the two grandchildren, Hannah Hargreaves and your own son, Dermot, also receive quite handsome bequests in your father's will.'

'Not compared with the three of us. And neither of the grandchildren was present when we tried to persuade Dad to move out of High Beeches.' Alan Fletcher's face had set stubbornly at the suggestion that his son might be close to this killing.

'Very well. So you're saying that all you three children had reason to hope that your father would see fit to help your various schemes. And now you are all substantial beneficiaries of his will, with no need to convince him any longer that your schemes are worthwhile.'

'Are you suggesting –'

'I'm not suggesting anything, Mr Fletcher. Just reiterating certain facts that we all need to keep in mind when investigating a callous murder. Whose idea was it that Walter Fletcher should move out of his home?'

Alan knew what the man was doing. Trying to rile him, to make him lose his cool. That mustn't happen. 'I told you. We all thought the same.'

'But these plans don't spring suddenly out of the air. Not as collective schemes. One of the three of you must have put the idea forward in the first place. Or four, if we include Jim Hargreaves, as I think we must.'

Alan licked his lips. He wished now that he had insisted on making tea. His whole mouth was drier than he could ever remember it being. 'I think it was Alison who first suggested it. But she discussed it with us to see whether we agreed. We were all involved in it.' He felt guilty about this. He must make sure Alison knew what he had said. Chris was right: they must keep each other in touch with what had been said to the police, and avoid contradicting each other. He was glad to feel his brother's intelligence behind them in this.

Lambert was thinking that if what this man was saying was true, they were a ruthless group – he noticed that Alan had not excluded Jim Hargreaves when offered the chance to do so. Plotting to persuade an old man to leave his house against his will. Yet from what they knew so far, Walter Fletcher's children seemed neither vicious nor without affection for the old man. Perhaps they just had strong reasons for wanting the money, which had made them behave irrationally. It was irrational, for there had been little chance of that vigorous father acceding to their scheme, according to Brenda Collins and Eve Brownrigg.

Alan Fletcher did not strike him as either vicious or ruthless as he studied him in that warm kitchen. Yet murder needed only a sudden moment of savagery, often from someone behaving out of previous character. Lambert said quietly, 'Why did you need your father's money, Mr Fletcher?'

So the moment was here at last, thought Alan. He had not expected the question to be put so baldly, but murder no doubt allowed them this directness. He took a deep breath, reminding himself of the words he had planned; never lie more than you have to, he had read somewhere. 'I need to develop this place. I had – still have – the chance of more land. Good land, an adjoining field. And I shall invest in more glass, in due course.'

Lambert looked automatically round the room, with its shabby furnishings, its haircord carpet that was almost in holes. 'You seem to have plenty of work out there, and you know what you're doing. Couldn't you have financed expansion from your profits, like other businesses?'

'I have other . . . responsibilities.' Alan hissed the sibilants of the word bitterly.

'A wife and child, yes.'

'I meant the wife. Dermot I could handle, if it wasn't for her.'

'Your wife takes more than you can afford?'

His laugh was almost a snarl. 'Much more. She had a cleverer lawyer than me, when the settlement was drawn up. Half the time, I seem to be working just for her and her new boyfriend. If I show a profit in the books, she takes a full half. It doesn't leave room for expansion.'

'And your son. He helps to keep you poor as well, I suppose.'

'No!' The word came like a stone across the table at

them. For five seconds after it, Alan Fletcher strove to control his breath after the sudden shout. 'Dermot's got his problems, God knows, but he hasn't sponged off me.'

'He's in custody at the moment, on drugs charges.'

Fletcher nodded, eyes on the scrubbed planks of the table. 'I know. In Birmingham – I was informed. I am still his next of kin, you know.'

At a nod from Lambert, Hook said gently, 'Your son must have given you a lot of worry over the last few years, Mr Fletcher.'

'He's not a bad lad. Not really.' Alan Fletcher looked up, suddenly anxious to convince them, a burly figure in grubby shirtsleeves and braces, with a smudge of soil on his forehead and a fragment of dead leaf in his ruffled hair. A man who was suddenly oozing love. 'When he was working here, he was perfectly all right. But there wasn't enough work for two of us, not with what she took.' His head jerked towards the wall on the words, as if the hated wife was in the next room. 'When I expand, Dermot will come back here and work. He'll be all right, then.'

Hook watched the man for a moment, vulnerable at last as he tried to convince them about his son. Eventually, Bert said softly, 'Dermot was also a beneficiary of your father's will, Mr Fletcher.'

It took a second or two for the implications of this to strike Fletcher. He had thought that Chris and Alison and he were the only ones the police would suspect. Now his dark-blue eyes widened in horror. 'It's not substantial, what Dermot gets. It's nothing, compared with what Chris and Alison and I get.'

'Nevertheless, your son receives a considerable sum, in young men's terms,' Hook insisted gently. In other circumstances, he would have been tempted to dwell on the difference fifty thousand pounds would make to his own life, but he was genuinely sympathetic to this father's concern for his boy. Bert had two sons of his own, with the trials of adolescence still to come.

Lambert, asserting his hard man's role in this improvised duet, said, 'I understand that one of your son's early crimes was to steal money from his grandfather.'

It was not strictly speaking a crime at all, of course, since there was no record of it, but he wanted to make the incident as serious as possible for the rattled father. Alan said harshly, 'Who told you that?'

'He told us himself, Mr Fletcher. In explaining why he was no longer on good terms with his grandfather at the time of this murder.'

So it came to this. You kept quiet about the boy's stealing from his grandfather, even persuaded your brother and sister to keep quiet. And then the lad went and told the police himself. Alan shook his head hopelessly, like a man who knows the truth but has no hope of convincing his listeners. 'Dermot didn't kill his grandfather.'

'You will understand that we cannot simply take your word for that, any more than we can take his. If you know anything that may help to eliminate him from our investigation, now is obviously the moment to reveal it.'

It was no more than a routine encouragement, the kind of sentence he had uttered hundreds of times over twenty years of CID work, but it seemed for a moment as if it might bring results. Alan Fletcher looked desperately from one to the other of his questioners. His chest heaved and he seemed about to shout something, but it would perhaps have been no more than another useless denial of his son's involvement.

Eventually his shoulders drooped and his gaze fell to the table. He reiterated hopelessly, 'Dermot would never have killed his granddad. I doubt whether he was even around at the time.'

He glanced across at the rug by the Aga, and Bella, as if in response, levered herself stiffly up and came across to put her muzzle in his hand. It was a slightly greying muzzle, but the brown eyes above it were bright and alert; after the initial stiffness in rising, the movement might have been that of a much younger dog. Lambert studied man and dog together for a moment, then said, 'Dermot takes the dog for walks, I believe.'

Fletcher looked at him as if it was an accusation. 'She's his dog. Always has been, since she came when he was thirteen,' he said. 'She gets plenty of exercise about this place, but I don't have time to take her out for walks.'

'So if she was seen near High Beeches, Bella would have been with your son.'

'I suppose so. It certainly wouldn't have been with me. I told you, I don't have time to walk her.' Alan fondled the dog's soft ears as its head rested against his knee, as if in compensation.

'Bella was up there with Dermot on the day before your father's death, the Monday, wasn't she?'

'She might have been. I can't remember now.' His sullenness was almost an admission in itself. Perhaps he realized it, for he roused himself to say defiantly, 'But that's the day before. It doesn't mean Dermot was at the house on the Tuesday.'

'Indeed not. However, I now have to tell you, Mr Fletcher, that we have two sightings of Bella reported near High Beeches on the day of your father's death.'

Alan Fletcher's face was aghast. It seemed to whiten as he looked from Lambert to the more sympathetic Hook with an unspoken agony. There was no relief to be had there: Hook responded only with a tiny, confirmatory nod.

It seemed Alan would say nothing, but he said eventually, without much conviction now, 'Dermot wasn't there. Whoever killed Dad, it wasn't him. You won't pin it on him.'

Hook found himself hoping unprofessionally that Alan Fletcher was right in this. They asked him about Christopher and Alison, but he parried the questions about his brother and sister with an ease he had not shown when his son was the subject. He was like a batsman with a secure defence now, thought ex-seam-bowler Hook, attempting little but showing few signs of discomfort either.

Basically, Alan acknowledged that his brother and sister

126

and his sister's husband all had motives like him, then found it inconceivable that any of them could have killed the old man. He denied all knowledge of their movements on that day, when he had worked resolutely on his chrysanths and tomatoes and on lifting the first winter cauliflowers from his plot at the sheltered end of his land.

At least the three children weren't giving alibis to each other, thought Lambert. He had half expected that they would be, but the absence of such collusion failed to cheer him. A concocted alibi might have offered a pointer to the source or sources of this bewildering evil.

Alan Fletcher, recovering noticeably after they moved off the subject of his son, managed to seem cooperative, even appropriately anxious to unearth the killer of his father during the rest of their exchanges. 'Helping the police with their enquiries'; Alan recalled the phrase, and thought in retrospect that he had not after all made such a bad job of the interview.

He gave himself a few minutes to collect his thoughts when they had left, and rang first Chris, then Alison. It was important, even in the areas where they were patently innocent, that they should present a united front to the police. It would cause all sorts of embarrassments if their statements disagreed in matters of detail.

Both brother and sister listened carefully to his account of his exchanges with the superintendent and sergeant. Alison checked his impressions off against hers; Chris was anxious to prepare himself for his own interview that afternoon, which he plainly thought would be an ordeal.

He made his elder brother repeat most of the things they had asked, until Alan found himself trying hard to reassure him. 'I don't think they really have much idea who did it, yet. They even seemed to think at one point that it might have been Dermot,' he said with a brittle laugh. 'So they really haven't much idea, have they?'

15

Lambert was snatching a sandwich in his own office when the news came through.

His door was open, so that he caught enough of the excitement in Rushton's voice. He was down the corridor and into the incident room before the DI had put the phone down.

Drama has its own momentum; even normally quiet men like to make the full impact it allows them. Rushton put down the phone, surveyed the expectant faces of Lambert and Hook and the other members of the team, and instinctively made the most of his moment.

'That was the buyer from Marks and Spencer's,' he said. 'We asked him to run a check on that sweater that Alison Hargreaves said she bought on the day when her father was killed.' He glanced automatically towards the labelled bag on the open shelves at the end of the room. Would the dark-green woollen within it, suddenly endowed with a new significance in these last few seconds, now be held aloft as an important exhibit in a celebrated trial?

'Well?'

Lambert's impatience hammered like a warning on the monosyllable. Rushton heeded it. 'We've got a result. The sweater certainly wasn't bought on that afternoon.'

'When, then?'

'They can't be precise. But each batch from the suppliers is labelled with a code number. The batch this garment belonged to was cleared from the store at least five weeks before Alison Hargreaves said she bought it. The manager is prepared to state in court that there is no way she could have bought it on that Tuesday afternoon.'

The sun made a belated appearance as they drove through the Forest, shining wanly through the autumn colours as Lambert's old Vauxhall passed among the high trees on the road to Cinderford.

Bert Hook had been silent for an unusually long period when he said, 'It doesn't necessarily mean that she did it. It only means that she wasn't where she told us she was on that afternoon.'

'Precisely. But she knew when the murder was committed and lied about her whereabouts at the time. Where the hell was Alison Hargreaves, if not at her father's house?'

'That is a question I shall take pleasure in asking her, in due course,' said Hook. He was always more affected when the lies came from a woman, particularly one of those middle-class women who had made so many decisions for him when he was a Barnardo's boy.

'A devious lot, these Fletcher children. It behoves us to give full attention to whatever the quietest of them has to tell us this afternoon,' said Lambert.

Hook thought of the ascetic features and physical frailty of Christopher Fletcher. In murder investigations, quiet men too often proved to have hidden depths of violence.

The working towns of the Forest usually surprised summer visitors by their dullness. Tourists tended to expect the picturesque Tudor gables and mellow stone of the photogenic Cotswold villages to the north east, and were accordingly disappointed. Cinderford was no Bourton-on-the-Water. But its inhabitants would have scorned the comparison.

Life around here had been hard for centuries, the place being the centre of the small mines that had sat for so long below the sheep and woods of the area. Cinderford, like the other towns of the Forest, reflected the grimness of the struggle for life, the small margins there had been between existence and starvation over the centuries.

Whether it was the ideal place to run a bookshop was another question altogether. W.H. Smith's did not think the town a big enough centre to warrant a shop, so that agent of competition at least was absent. But Fletcher Books was sandwiched between a central-heating specialist and a carpet shop whose windows were partly obscured by lurid posters proclaiming its autumn sale of kitchen vinyls.

The bookshop's narrow facade was not likely to attract attention or interest among those not committed to book-buying. Behind its grimy plate glass, there were the novels of the latest Booker shortlist and four substantial biographies. For the rest, the books on display were second-hand and without much apparent order. It was certainly not an eye-catching use of the limited window-space available.

The owner was as low-key as his premises. Chris Fletcher came round the counter to meet them, almost offered to shake hands, then decided that would be inappropriate. 'We can go through to my office,' he said. 'You may have to excuse me for a moment if a customer comes in, but this is usually a quiet time.'

Both his visitors wondered when the busy times occurred. The 'office' turned out to be what had been designed as the living quarters behind the shop. The walls were lined with cartons of books; Hook had to resist the temptation to walk across to an incomplete set of Wisdens, whose yellow bindings peeped through the torn cardboard.

A table and four dining chairs occupied the centre of the room, the last bastions of a domesticity which had all but disappeared. When the three sat down at this table, the policemen were reminded inevitably of the deal table where they had sat earlier in the day with this man's brother, Alan.

Yet the elder brother had been very much an outdoor man, chafing at the unaccustomed inactivity, whereas Christopher Fletcher seemed an indoor man, whose natu-

130

ral habitat might have been a major reference library or a museum.

An estate agent's sheet with a colour picture of Chepstow Castle was lying on the scratched surface of the table. Fletcher turned it over quickly, almost guiltily. It was his first mistake.

'Thinking of a move?' said Lambert casually. Detection allowed an inquisitiveness that would have been rudeness in a private exchange.

Chris Fletcher did not seem to mind, seemed in fact almost anxious to enlighten them. 'I'm considering a move to more suitable premises.' He looked round shamefacedly at his shabby surroundings, remembering how years ago he had protested the suitability of this place as a bookshop to parents anxious for him to do something more practical.

Lambert said, 'You were enquiring about bigger shops a month before your father died, we're told. Wasn't that rather anticipating his death?'

Lambert hoped to rattle the quiet, ascetic figure with the suggestion. Chris was shaken, but not surprised by such tactics. He shrugged his thin shoulders and said, through lips which were drier than he would have wished, 'I was hopeful of persuading Dad to help me, yes. Wanted more room, to spread my wings a bit.'

He had almost said 'our', he realized. It was a reminder to him of how careful he must be with these people.

'We spoke to your brother this morning.'

'Yes. He said you'd been.' He had been drawn into this reaction by the silence they had left for him, he realized. So much for his resolution to be careful. Now they knew that he and Alan had been in contact in the interval between these meetings. Chris felt as if he were already giving ground in this contest, even though no lines of battle had yet been defined.

'Indeed? Did he tell you that we'd been asking him about the movements of his son Dermot?'

'I – er – I think he did mention it, yes.' Chris was thrown

off balance by this. The last thing he had thought they would begin with was Dermot. A shaft of self-preservation pressed disconcertingly into Chris's brain. If they were after Dermot, his mind insisted selfishly, that must surely divert attention away from him. 'My nephew has had his troubles, over the last few years.'

Lambert nodded, a sober-faced Machiavelli. 'He is in custody at the moment in Birmingham, on rather serious drugs charges. Do you think he is capable of murdering his own grandfather?'

Again the abruptness of the suggestion caught Chris unready for it. He tried to gather his ideas, to present the cool, dispassionate front he had planned when he prepared himself for this afternoon. 'You really would know more about that than me, Superintendent. Murder is a thing we do not often meet in the book trade, except in a fictional context, of course. So –'

'We may have seen more murder than you have, Mr Fletcher, but we haven't seen young Mr Dermot Fletcher at all, though one of my team has interviewed him. I'm asking you to give us an opinion on an individual, that's all.'

Chris fought down a desire to be loyal to Alan, reminding himself of the need to keep his own concerns as remote as possible from this investigation. He tried not to think of Alan's fierce affection for Dermot as he said, 'I – I haven't seen very much of my nephew over the last five years or so. But I know he has been in trouble for most of them. They do say that one crime leads on to another, don't they?'

Chris found he felt excitement, not remorse, at his treachery. Remorse might come later in the day, when there would be time and room for it.

Lambert did not comment. Instead, he studied the thin face, with its frame of lank grey hair, as if he might find answers there. After a silence that was wholly disconcerting to the man under scrutiny, he said, 'Dermot Fletcher had fallen out with your father. Probably he knew that he was a substantial beneficiary under the will. Fifty thousand pounds is a lot of money for a desperate young man, with a mind confused by drugs. Do you think he could have killed your father?'

'He would have been capable of it, I suppose.' Chris felt the power of independent thought ebbing away as the instinct for self-protection pulsed through him. He dropped his gaze to the table, avoiding the intensity of Lambert's grey, unblinking eyes.

'How close are you to your nephew, Mr Fletcher?'

'I haven't talked much with Dermot lately. But when we last spoke – it must have been at Christmas or New Year – he seemed to have lost the sense of moral distinction, to have no very clear delineation of right and wrong in his mind.' Chris concentrated upon a scratch on the table, picking his way carefully through the words, as if the right semantics could cloak his treachery. 'But that could be partly a result of drug dependency, I suppose.'

Lambert said nothing. It was perfectly true that one result of drugs could be a blurring of moral certainties, but acknowledging that might put this nervous creature a little more at his ease. He watched the slender hands twisting and untwisting on the scratched table by the agent's brochure. Chris Fletcher's blue eyes darted from him to Hook and back again, anxious for any reassurance that his words were being taken seriously.

Eventually, Lambert said, 'The boy was near your father's house on the day before he was killed. That has been established. And the dog – I forget its name – was seen near High Beeches on the day of the murder.'

'Bella. She and Dermot are inseparable, when he's around.' Suddenly, when it seemed they were about to tell him that Dermot was going to be charged, Chris felt ashamed of his eagerness to implicate his nephew.

Lambert glanced down for no more than a second at the brochure beneath Fletcher's hand. 'Did you get on well with your father?' he said.

It was a bewildering switch, back to where Chris had

expected the questioning to start. He had known he would be asked this, yet now he found himself unready for it. 'We got on well – very well, I think – when I was young. We weren't as close in these last few years, since my mother died.'

Lambert seemed to be hearing this from all the family. Had the dead woman acted as a buffer between children and a dictatorial father? Had the old man become more suspicious and less responsive to them as he had become elderly and lonely, as Brenda Collins had suggested? Or were these enigmatic Fletcher children merely disguising forms of disagreement between themselves and the dead man?

They were comparing notes about their meetings with him and the rest of the team. That might indicate no more than a normal family closeness. Or it might suggest that they had conspired in the old man's murder, and were now conspiring to frustrate the investigation of it.

But the daughter, Alison, had already lied to them about her whereabouts at the time of the murder, and her husband had been trying to hide something, as he was pretty sure this man was. And Alan Fletcher, who had as yet no alibi for the time of the murder, had almost admitted that his son was near the scene of the killing on the day. The idea of some sort of conspiracy amongst this irritating family became more attractive by the minute.

Lambert made it sound as much of an accusation as he could when he said, 'Your father died early in the afternoon of Tuesday, twenty-third October. Where were you at that time, Mr Fletcher?'

Deliver it casually, Chris told himself. It doesn't matter if it sounds like a prepared statement, because they will expect you to have thought about the answer to such a routine question. He could not rid his throat of a hoarseness as he said, 'I was here in the shop. Early-closing day here is Wednesday, so I was open all afternoon.'

'Is there anyone who can support this for you?'

'There would be customers, of course. But I'm not sure –'

'Mr Fletcher, what would be your reaction if I told you we have someone who is prepared to state, in court if that should eventually be necessary, that you were away for two hours on that afternoon, that you shut up the shop and left a handwritten note on the door to say that you would be back at three p.m.?'

It was suddenly very quiet in that untidy box of a room. Chris Fletcher looked into the two watchful, experienced faces, and his own thought processes were laid bare. They could see him preparing to deny it, weighing the chances of success, then deciding it was hopeless. It seemed a long time before his thin shoulders drooped and he said hopelessly, 'All right. I wasn't here at that time. But I didn't kill Dad. Even when he was being awkward, I loved him.'

The simple declaration dropped unexpectedly from the lips of this diffident, intellectual figure. If Lambert felt any satisfaction that in the complicated world of this investigation someone should declare a simple, undiluted love for the victim, he gave no sign of it. He said, 'Then we shall need to know where you were at the time when he was killed. And why you have just chosen to lie to us.'

'That's private. It has nothing to do with this.' Fletcher's refusal was instinctive, unthinking.

'On the contrary, it has everything to do with it. If you were with someone else, he or she will be able to confirm that, and eliminate you from this enquiry. Assuming, of course, that we find them more reliable in their account than you have been.'

'I went to see someone in Gloucester. A – a close friend.'

'Good. Name and address, please.'

It was being distorted, Chris thought. The whole relationship was soiled, being dragged out like this. Torn from him by these strangers, when he had concealed it so long and so determinedly from his own family. He said, 'I want the person kept out of this. We – we're going to live together, once all this is over.'

135

Chris gestured vaguely round the room, as if the whole of his present life would drop away with the conclusion of the murder enquiry. As it would, of course. With the money which was coming and the partner who was going to share it, he would have a life he could never have envisaged, even a few months ago.

Lambert said wearily, 'We need this person's name, Mr Fletcher, whoever she may be.'

Chris was suddenly furious with this persistent figure with the grizzled hair and laser eyes. Why on earth should he presume it was a woman? Anger made Chris careless of what he had striven so long to conceal. 'It isn't a woman. Can't you people understand anything except the obvious?'

Lambert concealed his elation that at last he had provoked indiscretion in this cautious and intelligent figure. 'Your sexual predilections are no concern of ours, Mr Fletcher. Unless they have a bearing upon our investigation, of course.' He hoped they would be spared the usual stuff about discovering one's sexuality, but did not voice that thought. 'We shall need the name of your partner.'

Chris's heart leapt at that word. He had thought always of the first revelation being to the family, and had braced himself for the shock and the arguments. These men seemed to accept it as a normal part of their day.

He had kept the knowledge of Phil and himself so secret for so long that he could scarcely credit this casual, thrilling acceptance of the two of them as a couple. 'His name is Philip Baker. I – I haven't even told the family about it yet. I couldn't, while Dad was around, you see, and there just doesn't seem to have been the right moment since then.'

'Your father wouldn't have approved, I take it?'

'No. He was what I always think of as an Old Testament Christian. We've had our rows in the past, when I became an agnostic in my youth, but he'd got used to that. But he'd never have been able to accept that I was homosexual.' Phil would have said 'gay'. He must get used to the term himself, now that he was going to be open about it at last.

'Your father had no inkling of this relationship.'

'No.'

'Had he known of it, might he have felt strongly enough to cut you out of his will?'

'He would have. There's no doubt of that. He just wasn't rational about what he called queers.' Chris stopped abruptly, aware too late that in his haste to explain his secrecy he had confessed to an ideal motive for murder.

Lambert looked at him coolly, watching that perception steal over his features. 'So your father's death came at a most opportune moment for you, Mr Fletcher. You could not have concealed this relationship for very much longer.'

'I wouldn't have wanted to!' Again this middle-aged intellectual leapt in like a young lover to assert the strength of his passion. Again the realization dawned that his words were incriminating. His hands sprang apart on the scratched table, and he looked from one to the other of his interrogators, like an animal contemplating a run for freedom. Then his shoulders slumped and he said in a monotone, 'You're right, of course. Once Dad had found out, he wouldn't have left me a penny.'

Lambert studied him for a moment. Fletcher's sensitive features were full of a mixture of pride and apprehension, his thin torso slumped in something near to exhaustion after the stress of his revelations. Murder stripped people bare, allowing no hiding place for the raw passions which might or might not have led them into desperate violence. He said, 'We'd better have the address of this Philip Baker, so that we can confirm the time of your meeting on that day.'

'It won't help. I wasn't with him during the early afternoon.' Fletcher's voice was so low that they strained to hear it in the quiet room.

Hook, poised over his notebook, wondered if a confession was coming. When no further words came from the man who now sat with his head in his hands, he said, 'So where were you, Mr Fletcher?'

It seemed a long time before the man spoke. Eventually Chris took his hands from his head and laid them with elaborate care on the table in front of him, as though they were inanimate objects which were not connected to him. With an effort of will, he raised his troubled, slate-blue eyes to look at his questioners.

Then he said, 'I intended to go and see Dad, to tell him about Philip and me. I drove over there – I'm surprised you haven't had sightings of the van reported. But as I moved up the valley towards High Beeches, I realized how hopeless it was. I told you: Dad just wouldn't have been prepared to listen. I stopped for a few minutes in the gate-way to a field, then turned the van and went back. I did meet Phil, to tell him what had happened, but that was later in the day.'

At least now, Chris thought amidst his distress, Phil won't have to lie for me, as he said he would.

In the shop, the bell on the door rang suddenly, as a customer belatedly reminded them of that other, normal world outside. Lambert went out, leaving the door not quite shut. They heard him telling the unseen patron that Mr Fletcher would be available in a few minutes.

Hook, writing furiously, said, 'Did you go right up to the house?'

'No. That gate was the nearest I got. It's on the lane which leads to Dad's. Perhaps quarter of a mile short of the house.'

Lambert came back in as Hook concluded his record of the details. It was when the interview was apparently complete that Fletcher said, 'I can tell you one thing. Dermot was up there that day. I saw Bella on the field footpath, not half a mile from High Beeches. Dermot is the only one who ever walks her up there.'

This echoed so exactly what the boy's own father had

138

said that it sounded an even more chilling note than his uncle realized.

Except, as Hook pointed out as they drove away from the Forest, that the information came from Christopher Fletcher, who had now admitted that he himself had been alone in the area at exactly the time of this murder.

16

The silence which falls over the Forest of Dean at night is profound. Nine out of ten people in Britain do not experience anything like it, for they live too near to cities or towns to feel this velvet calm.

It is a country silence, amidst a deep country darkness. The sounds which occasionally break into it, such as the screech of an owl or the bleat of a lamb, can be heard a mile away, but they emphasize rather than diminish the quiet. After each of these noises, reminders that the darkness conceals not a dead but a living world, the silence floods softly back, wrapping itself round the listener until it seems a tangible thing.

The three people who moved through the Forest darkness to their meeting were all well used to the silence of the place at night; they had known it from childhood. And they journeyed through it to that oasis of light and warmth, an English village pub.

Endean was little more than a hamlet, half the size that it had been a century earlier, when farm labourers had still thronged the area. But because it was remote it had kept its precious village shop, when larger communities had lost theirs. And its church and its pub survived, though its tiny school had long since ceased to cater for the shrinking numbers of children. The church was served now by a vicar based elsewhere, but the King's Head, with a local clientele supplemented by summer and weekend visitors in cars, maintained a modest prosperity.

When he suggested to his brother and sister that they

should meet here, Alan Fletcher had forgotten that it was the place where his father's funeral day had been concluded. It had simply seemed the most convenient place, once they had agreed on the phone that they would not meet in any of their houses. Two of them came on foot. Alison had only half a mile to walk, and he had perhaps twice that distance. It was true that he would normally have driven there to save time, but they had agreed that vehicles might attract attention to their meeting, when they wished it to remain undiscovered.

Only Chris Fletcher came there on wheels, turning his old van into the overflow car park at the back of the inn where it would not be noticed, even though at this hour in the early evening there was plenty of room on the old cobbles in front of the building. As he locked the van and pulled his coat collar about his ears against the autumn cold, he could not resist the thought that there was something conspiratorial about this meeting of a murder victim's three children.

Alison and Alan were already there when he went into the sudden brightness of the inn, sitting at the far end of the long room where the reception had been held after the funeral. It gave a bizarre setting to this meeting, despite the newly lit fire which flamed cheerfully in the old brick fireplace beside them. He was sure the other two were also aware of the last time they had been here.

Alan got him a half of bitter from the bar, nodding at the two regulars who sat talking on stools, and set it alongside the other two drinks on the small table. Chris took a large mouthful, savouring the sharp taste in his throat, watching Alan pull appreciatively at his pint, reminded of his older brother's buying him his first beer a quarter of a century ago, in this very place.

'I thought we should compare notes,' said Alan, unnecessarily. They all knew why they had come. He was an uneasy chairman, but he was the eldest, and all three of them expected him to assume the role. 'The police might be watching our houses, making notes of who comes and goes, so it seemed best that we should meet here.'

It was a bizarre notion, a situation which a month ago none of them would have expected ever to encounter. Yet there seemed nothing strange to them now in his words. If they were behaving like guilty creatures, that was what murder and the consequent police investigation had brought them to.

'They might well be watching me,' said Alison unexpectedly. 'They caught me out in a lie, you see. I said I was in Gloucester buying a sweater at the time Dad died – I thought it would leave me in the clear with the police. But apparently they can tell when you buy things at Marks and Spencer's these days.'

She gave them a wan smile. She was as trim as usual, the brooch in the chiffon scarf at her throat sparkling as it caught the firelight, the deep-green sweater perfectly complementing the helmet of dark hair which framed her face. But that face showed the strain of the last two weeks. The features were more pinched than they remembered them, the crow's-feet around the eyes too deep for make-up. The bright, almost black eyes were as observant as ever, but strained with the effort of their vigilance.

She did not say where she had been on that fatal afternoon, but neither of them even thought of asking her. It was unthinkable that Alison, the laughing girl they had grown up with, who had been lovingly protected by Alan and who had herself been the guardian of delicate young Chris, should have been at High Beeches that day, should have sent the father they had all loved plunging to his death.

Instead, Alan said, 'You can tell them you were here with me if you like, sis.'

It was years since he had used the diminutive, and both of them felt the intimacy of the moment. Alison said, 'But they'll already have asked you about that.'

He smiled, trying hard to relax her, to be the elder brother she needed now as she had not done for years. 'I told them I was at home, that was all. You could have been there with me. They might not like me withholding that information when they talked to me, but they can't do much about that. We were none of us on oath, after all. And I didn't kill Dad, so there's no way helping you can affect me.'

For Alan Fletcher, it was quite a long speech, and he enjoyed the sensation of taking charge. He was not normally a sensitive man, but the empathy between brother and sister had been strong since childhood. It felt good to reassert it in this crisis. He smiled at her again, a smile that said, 'Don't tell me where you really were, if you don't want to in front of Chris. We can compare notes later.'

Alison's mind was racing ahead, trying and failing to see snags in an arrangement which would enable her to protect the one man she really cared about. She sat for a moment with a hand at each side of her head, concentrating as hard as if she had been alone in the room. Then she said, 'Thanks, Alan. If you think it won't compromise you, I'll tell them that when they come back to me tomorrow.'

Chris Fletcher looked from his sister's drawn face to the fire. He wanted to say that these CID policemen were clever men, that more lies would only result in more trouble. But in this family setting, he had never been the leader, always the led.

So instead of offering advice he said, 'They caught me out as well.' He had not thought to tell them about this, but the need to reassure Alison that she was not alone was taking over. He told the two surprised faces, 'I said I was in the shop on the afternoon when Dad was killed, but the police asked around the street. I suppose I should have expected that. I'd left a note on the door saying I was out, and someone told them about it.'

Alan looked at him sharply. 'Where were you, Chris?'

None of them thought it odd that he should ask Chris that, when he had not pressed Alison about her whereabouts. Chris found he was glad he could answer them without telling them about Phil. He had come here meaning to tell them at last, but now the atmosphere seemed wrong. He didn't want to toss his precious relationship into this grim little meeting. There would be other, more suitable, times, after this nightmare had been concluded.

So he now said simply, 'I was up here. Near Dad's. I drove the van up, intending to see Dad, to try to sort things out, after the row we'd had on Sunday.' And to try to keep myself in his will, after he knew about Phil, he thought. But he held that bit back. He wasn't telling them lies, just holding back a little of the truth. They would understand how difficult it had been for him, once they knew about Phil.

Alan was looking at him sharply. 'You went up to High Beeches on that Tuesday afternoon?'

'Not quite. I stopped in the gate to Noakes's hayfield. Decided I couldn't face Dad after all, so I turned back there.' Alison's bright eyes seemed even wider; Alan's face was full of what might even be horror. They knew the place he meant exactly; they had walked past it every day for years on the way home from school.

Chris felt the palms of his hands suddenly wet and cold. Surely they couldn't think that he wasn't telling them the truth, that he'd done this awful thing?

Alan glanced towards the distant bar, checking that they were still unobserved. He turned slightly to face his brother, his big shoulders suddenly menacing to the younger man. 'How long were you there, Chris?'

'Scarcely at all. I realized how impossible it was and turned back.' Chris cut down a little on the time he had sat hopelessly in the car. And he hadn't mentioned seeing Bella up there. Of course! That was why Alan was so on edge. He knew Dermot had been up there that day and was wondering if anyone else had seen him.

Chris decided that he wouldn't mention seeing the dog on the footpath. He wished now that he hadn't told the police. He was suddenly brimming with sympathy for his brother and the life he had had. Working away like a slave on that field, and for what? First for a wife who had been nothing but trouble for him, and now for this lad, who was going from bad to worse.

Alan looked at the anxious faces on each side of him, waiting it seemed for a lead. He said heavily, 'They're a clever pair, that superintendent and his sidekick. Bert Hook, he's called, the sergeant. I played cricket against him once, in the old days.' Those old days seemed at that moment immensely attractive to all of them.

For Alan, they were long ago, when he was not even married, and these two were youngsters, looking to him for guidance, in a world which seemed much simpler than this one. He said, 'Well, I take it we're agreed that it was none of us who killed Dad?'

Alison gave a nervous little giggle, turning it into an agreement. They all wished he hadn't put it so bluntly, or hadn't put it at all, but words had never been Alan's strongest point. Chris said, 'That goes without saying, Alan.' His smile did not come from within; it sat on that grave countenance like something externally applied.

Alison said, 'If we didn't kill him, who did?' She looked at them both, noting the little shakes of the head, forcing them to go on with this idea. 'The police are checking on the grandchildren, you know. Hannah's all right, because she was at the university, in lectures. But they've checked that out with other students.'

She was glad now that they had, because her daughter was in the clear through their efforts. Alison tried not to reveal the satisfaction she felt in that thought.

Alan nodded. 'They seemed to think it might have been Dermot when they spoke to me. Because he gets fifty thousand, you know. Dad never got round to cutting him out of his will.' It was the first time he had acknowledged the intention in his father to punish his grandson for his transgressions. 'But it wasn't Dermot. He wasn't around at the time of Dad's murder.'

Chris, who thought he knew otherwise, did not comment on that. Instead, he said, 'They pressed me a little about Dermot. But if he didn't do it, they can't pin it on him, can they?' It sounded in his own ears defensive, as if he was seeking reassurance from the other two.

But Alan only said again, 'He wasn't here, so he couldn't have done it.' It was as though he felt that if he repeated the notion often enough, the wish might become fact.

Alison said diffidently, 'There's my husband, of course. But Jim was safely in school at the time of the killing, thank goodness.'

She thought of him, sitting where she had left him at home, brown eyes half closed in his tired face beneath the thinning hair. He would not have moved from that armchair. Probably he would be asleep by now, with the television droning unheard in front of him.

Even now, she thought, Jim Hargreaves was an outsider, after twenty years and more. These two brothers of hers excluded people born outside the Forest almost as completely as their father had done. Jim should really have been at this meeting with them, but they had never even thought of inviting him.

Well, that mattered less now to her than it would once have done. For a moment, she wondered whether she should tell them now that Jim might not be so important to her, in the future. Then she realized that Chris was speaking.

'What about Brenda Collins?' he said. 'She lives very near to Dad's house, and she could easily have got up there without being noticed.'

The jolly widow, plump and unashamed of it, cheerful and direct, was the kind of woman Chris had never been able to deal with. Even as a child, he had been in awe of the blonde and buxom Mrs Collins, when other boys had enjoyed crude adolescent fantasies about her curves. Even as an adult, he had been uncomfortable with her comfortings after his mother's death, and certainly suspicious of her closeness to his father in the succeeding years.

146

Alison was aware of this. Some deep-seated loyalty to her sex made her want to defend Brenda, though she had been as resentful as her brothers of the woman's closeness to their dead father. She said, 'But what could Brenda gain from Dad's death? If we were right about Dad being soft on her, she might have married him in due course, and stood to gain much more.'

Chris was reluctant to let the idea go. He said, 'But suppose we were wrong? She's always denied that she and Dad were going to marry, and sometimes I think Dad just enjoyed having us think they might. Perhaps she wanted the money now, not at some vague time in the future.'

Alan said, 'Dad was down at her house on the day before he died. We don't know what happened between them then. Suppose he told her he was going to cut her out of the will, for some reason? She knew he was going to be working up the ladder on that Tuesday, because he was full of his plans to paint the house. Anyone could have knocked him off that ladder, you know.'

'Even a woman, you mean,' said Alison wryly.

Chris grinned at her, his face lighting up with a boyish mischief, as she had not seen it do for months. 'Or a chap with a gammy leg,' he said.

Alan was too preoccupied to join in the joke. He said, 'There's Eve Brownrigg, you know. She gets ten thousand from Dad's will. It's a hell of a lot for her. More than she's ever had in her life. And she could use it, with old Charlie in a wheelchair.'

'She was good to Dad,' said Alison. She was suddenly full of sympathy for the ageing, bow-legged figure who had appeared faithfully on two mornings a week to clean High Beeches. 'Eve Brownrigg wouldn't have killed him, surely? She seemed very fond of Dad.'

'Someone who seemed fond of him killed him,' said Alan doggedly. 'All I'm saying is that she must be considered. She was the last person known to have seen him alive, apparently. Says she left him an hour or two before he was killed.'

'She certainly had the best opportunity of all,' agreed Chris judicially. He couldn't believe that old Eve Brownrigg could have killed his father, but it was good to sound objective. And it cheered him to spread the net beyond the family, after what the police had put him through earlier in the day.

'I'll drop in and see them during the week,' said Alison. 'See if Charlie gives anything away. He's so glad to see you that he always talks. And we know them so much better than the police – he might be less on his guard with me, if they have anything to hide.'

'I'll ask around the village about Brenda Collins,' said Alan as they broke up. The prospect of action, of initiating their own enquiries after being so thoroughly investigated themselves, was curiously cheering. 'Perhaps we can compare notes again at the end of the week.'

None of them knew as they went out into the darkness that events were moving much faster than that.

17

At the same time as the children of Walter Fletcher were meeting at the King's Head in Endean, a man made his way reluctantly towards the police station in Oldford.

At this hour in the early evening, he could have parked near the austere new municipal building. Instead, he chose to park two hundred yards away and walk slowly through the side streets to his goal, as if even at this late stage he wanted time to review the morality of his actions.

But his resolution held. He moved through the big double doors to the long barrier of the desk, where the station sergeant was well used to dealing with the diffident. The sergeant sized up this tousled figure; late forties; educated; uncertain; unused to police stations.

A member of the public, perhaps, trying to do his duty in a way the media increasingly portrayed as old-fashioned. A crackpot, equally possibly. But when visitors mentioned murder and identified the case to you at the desk, you passed them on to CID. Smartly.

Sergeant Johnson said politely, 'If you'll take a seat for a moment, sir, I'll get someone working on the case to come and speak to you.'

Lambert was on his way out of the building. He had spent an hour on his own reviewing the case, trying to see some sort of pattern in the mass of material they had assembled so quickly over the last few days. Now he cursed himself for not going home earlier.

But when Johnson came through on the internal phone, he said immediately, 'I'll see him myself.' It was curiosity, not conscience, which drove him. He would have wondered all night what the man had to say if he had walked past him in the waiting area.

He sat the man in the single armchair in his office. For once, he was even glad to be without Bert Hook and his notebook; from the look of this nervous visitor, it would be best to keep things as informal as possible. He said, 'I'm in charge of the case you mentioned. The murder of Walter Fletcher.'

The man nodded, reassured rather than inhibited by the mention of the word 'murder', which stopped so many people in their tracks. He said, 'It's because it's a serious crime that I'm here. My name is Marsden. Simon Marsden. I work at the Forest of Dean Secondary School.'

It was the first clue about the reason for his presence on this cold November evening. The name struck a chord in Lambert's memory, but Marsden pinpointed the area before he could search it out for himself. 'I teach English there. One of my colleagues is Jim Hargreaves.'

'I see. You will probably be aware, then, that we have questioned Mr Hargreaves in connection with this investigation.'

'He said he'd been "helping you with your enquiries". Along with others, I'm sure.' His little attempt to lighten the atmosphere did not come off, because it did not dispel his own nervousness.

'Along with many others. But no doubt you are here because of Mr Hargreaves.'

'I – I don't want this to go any further, if it can be avoided.'

'If that can be avoided, it will be, Mr Marsden.' Lambert felt his impatience rising: it had been a long and gruelling day. But this was a member of the public who had come forward voluntarily to try to help them.

'It's – well, it's about that Tuesday afternoon when this apparently happened.'

'When an elderly man was flung from the top of a ladder and left to die in a pool of his own blood, yes, Mr

Marsden.' There was no harm in reminding diffident people of the brutality of the starting-point in these things.

With Simon Marsden, it worked. He nodded, casting aside his reservations in that moment. 'I understand Jim told you that he was in school that afternoon. At the time of the murder, I mean.'

Lambert's brain ran back over several days, to the interview with Jim and Alison Hargreaves at their house in Endean. They had tended since to concentrate on Alison, because of her lie about the purchase of her sweater in Gloucester, but there were moments when her husband had also seemed uncertain of himself. 'He told us that, indeed, Mr Marsden. Are you saying that he lied to us?'

For a moment he thought he had been too direct. But Marsden had gone too far now to withdraw. He ran a hand quickly through his luxuriant brown hair, hesitated for a moment, and said, 'He was in the school at the beginning and end of the afternoon. But he had the first two periods of the three free. He was out of the school then. I don't know where he went.'

Simon Marsden came out with all the facts at once. He was like one of his pupils, Lambert thought wryly: having brought himself to speak, he tumbled everything out quickly, as if anxious to get it over with as briefly as possible. Lambert paused for a moment, making sure that the staccato flow of information had ceased, then asked calmly, 'For how long was Mr Hargreaves out of the school?'

'About an hour and a half, I think. He left before afternoon school began at two. He must have been back by three-twenty, to teach the last period.'

'There are lies all round us,' Hook said sourly to Rushton at nine o'clock on the next morning. The DI looked up from his computer, dragging himself back from other, minor cases to this major one.

Very soon, Bert Hook would have to react to the new knowledge Marsden had brought to them. But first, in a rare moment of self-indulgence, he would sound off about the policeman's lot; had he not been asked to put DI Rushton in the picture?

He allowed his Gloucestershire indignation full rein as he counted off his complaints on his fingers. 'We caught Chris Fletcher out yesterday. God knows whether his new tale is the truth: he admits that he was near his father's house at the time of the murder, and there's no one to support his contention that he turned back without seeing the old man. Alan, the elder brother, tells us he was at home at the time, but there's no one available to substantiate that. Then his sister Alison spins us this yarn about being in Marks and Spencer's in Gloucester on that afternoon. Now we find her husband wasn't in school at the time – the one bloke we thought was safely in the clear.' The sergeant shook his head and stumped off to the phone.

Bert enjoyed putting the school secretary at the Forest of Dean Secondary School in her place. She sounded on the phone like the kind of petty bureaucrat who had dictated his life at Barnardo's for years. No appointments with staff without prior permission from the head teacher, she said firmly. And she would certainly need to know the nature of their business. 'That you cannot have, madam,' said Hook officiously. 'We are investigating a serious crime and you must realize that it is your duty to assist us.'

She capitulated quickly then. Mr Hargreaves would be free from teaching for forty minutes at ten-thirty. She would tell him to expect Superintendent Lambert and Sergeant Hook at that time. No, she supposed it wasn't in order for her to know what this was about. No, she certainly wouldn't tell anyone else about their visit. Yes, she would inform the head, if that was in order. Thank you, Sergeant.

Bert stared at the phone with a satisfied smile. One needed these little triumphs occasionally, to carry one along in a wicked world.

*   *   *

152

Alison Hargreaves said firmly, 'I was with my brother.' She wore no make-up on this bright, cold morning, as if to stress that all deceptions were now at an end.

'Then why didn't you tell us this earlier, instead of concocting this story about being in Gloucester?'

She took her time. What she had planned to say must not emerge too smoothly: this lying was a more difficult business than she had realized. 'I wasn't proud of my meeting with Alan. Neither was he, I think.'

It was warm in the Hargreaves home; the rooms were small and low-ceilinged, and the heating was turned up high. But Alison was shaken by a tiny, isolated shiver, as though in revulsion at the avarice which she perceived in her conduct.

Lambert looked at that naked face, so carefully blank. Her frame of hair looked even more severe round those clean, inscrutable features. She sat upright upon her chair, close enough to them for a faint scent of soap to reach them from the hands she clasped on her lap. She seemed as still and composed as a nun behind convent walls.

Except that Lambert still felt she was lying. He studied her for seconds before he said, 'Why did you meet your brother?'

'We met to see what could be done about the row we'd had with Dad on Sunday.'

'You wanted to patch things up?'

'Not exactly. We were discussing how we could still persuade Dad to part with some of his money. That's what I was ashamed of – especially when we found ourselves dragged into an investigation of his murder. Alan would have been prepared to tell you that I was there with him, but I didn't want it.'

It was convincing enough, in its way. If you said you were plotting to separate an old man from his money, it didn't sound a very praiseworthy story when you were accounting for your movements at the time of his murder. Perhaps it was natural she should have been reluctant to confess such plotting.

Her eyes had been cast down as she spoke. Now she looked up at him, desperate to be believed. 'We both had such pressing needs for the money, you see.'

That, at any rate, he believed. Alan's were obvious enough, in the light of the calls upon him from his absent wife and his errant son. Perhaps Alison's uses for the money she now had went beyond her husband's declared wish to set up a private school. But he knew she would not reveal them, and there were limits to how hard he could push her. She could legitimately refuse to discuss what she intended to do with what was now her own money.

They warned her that they would probably be back. She did not offer to see them out, and they left her sitting motionless in the stifling room.

They moved down the path that led through a neat cottage garden that might have come from an earlier, more ordered age. As they shut the gate and made for the car, they could see her profile through the wide window of the lounge. Hook wondered how long she would sit there before she moved.

As they drove through the quiet village of Endean, past the shut doors of the King's Head, Lambert made a decision. 'Get a tail put on our Mrs Hargreaves,' he said. 'Perhaps we'll find out exactly what it is she's trying to conceal.'

Dermot Fletcher looked gaunt and ill. It was a necessary stage in the treatment for drug dependence which had already begun in prison.

The magistrate asked if he wanted to sit rather than stand in the witness box. But he chose to stand, his thin white hands grasping the polished wood in front of him like the claws of a huge bird. He was very still during the brief period of his case, but the dark eyes were alert within their deep sockets, as they had not been a week earlier.

Dealing in drugs was a serious charge, and he would go to prison in due course. But this morning's proceedings

154

were little more than a formality, to establish that there was a case to answer in a higher court than this. It was confirmed that Dermot Fletcher was fit to plead. Then the case was passed on formally to the county court. Dermot was remanded in custody.

He was physically weak, and suffering much as his fixes became less frequent, in accordance with the programme the medics had laid down for him. The withdrawal symptoms were acute as the minutes dragged agonizingly slowly towards the time of his next allowance of cocaine.

But his brain was becoming clearer and his memory more reliable, day by day. And Dermot Fletcher was more and more concerned by his recollections of the days around his grandfather's death.

The school secretary was on the lookout for them. Even in a school where most of the teachers still dressed formally, the two large CID men in their grey suits stood out as they came through the reception area.

'Mr Hargreaves thought the best place would be in the Geography Room,' she said. She bustled efficiently ahead of them, up a double staircase, down a long corridor, past a series of classroom doors, enjoying the curious stares this strange trio attracted from pupils and staff.

Jim Hargreaves had set up chairs for them in the little storeroom he now regarded as his den. He was nervous, not less so because he thought he knew why Lambert and Hook had sought him out like this. They watched him bringing the kettle back to the boil, rattling teacups, adding sugar and milk as they directed. He was like an actor glad of a little business to make him less self-conscious in his movements. He improvised a little small talk about the weather and the school, as he waited for the principals to initiate the scene itself.

They seemed in no hurry, and he felt more than ever on stage and under observation as he sat down with them at the dusty table in the narrow room. The walls were lined with sets of textbooks and there were no windows;

the fluorescent light above them showed their faces in shadowless detail.

Lambert said, 'You told us when we saw you in your home that you were here in the school at the time when Walter Fletcher was killed. We have now been given reason to believe that you left the school for a lengthy spell on that afternoon.'

There it was. Couched in formal, even magisterial phrases by this watchful officer. Simon Marsden had split on him, then. It might not have been that, of course – someone might have seen him that day, and reported it. But he knew it was Marsden, as surely as he knew that he should never have relied on his friend to alibi him.

Jim felt no anger: it had been unfair of him to draw Simon in like that, without telling him what it involved. Simon had almost told him as much the other day. He might be a good teacher, Simon, but he hadn't the nerve for this.

Jim ran a palm over his thinning hair, letting his fingers feel the contours of his skull, which was now so thinly covered. His brown eyes were bright; the tight mouth was even threatening a smile of relief. He said, with a sigh which held no grief, 'You're right, I'm afraid. I did go out.'

It was almost the relief of confession. Lambert said with a touch of irritation, 'You've lied to us once, Mr Hargreaves. That is a more serious transgression than you appreciate, perhaps. Please do not try to deceive us again.'

It was a touch pompous. Curiously, that seemed to give Jim confidence; perhaps he realized that they were not quite so omniscient as they had seemed when they first came into his den. He said, 'I'm sorry I didn't tell you the truth at first. You're right, of course. I got my priorities wrong.'

'So where were you?'

'I went to the Halifax Building Society, to discuss commercial loans. I wanted to know how much money of our own we'd need to use as deposit on premises to convert

156

into a private school. I had a discussion with the local manager.'

'Time?' This was Bert Hook, determinedly neutral in tone, ballpoint pen at the ready.

'Two p.m. I left here at ten to, before afternoon school began. I was free for the first two periods, you see. But I expect you know that, now.'

'You weren't back here until after three.'

'No. About quarter past, I think. I remember being worried, because I'd cut it quite fine. I was teaching in here at twenty past.'

'So where else did you go?'

'I – well, I indulged myself, I'm afraid. It seemed that if we got the money we were hoping for from my father-in-law, we'd have more than enough for the deposit. So the plan was feasible. I drove round to look at the outsides of a couple of big old houses that we'd already noted as possibilities for the school. Permitted myself a little fantasy, I suppose.'

Lambert looked at him. He was sure they now had the truth. But it was a strange trip for a man to make when his hopes of the requisite funds should have been dashed two days previously. Had Jim Hargreaves been anticipating a murder and an inheritance?

Hargreaves seemed altogether too relaxed for a man caught out in his original statement. But the superintendent had known disturbed minds which positively enjoyed a few sharp rallies with the CID. Often they had been accompanied by a talent for ruthless violence. He said, 'I want you to consider your answer to this question carefully. Have you any idea who might have killed your father-in-law?'

'None whatsoever, Superintendent. Except that it wasn't me, of course.' This time he did permit himself a genuine smile. It lit up his eyes, extended to all his features. The idea, after all, was so ridiculous.

They were at the door when Hook said, 'This building

society – the Halifax, you said. Did you have an appointment?'

'Two o'clock. A Mr Ensten. I'm sure he'll confirm it for you.' He walked with them to the door of his classroom, for all the world like a benevolent host at the door of his house. 'You can find your own way out of this labyrinth?'

As they left the school, Lambert was confident that the manager would confirm the appointment. But Hargreaves would have had an hour after that meeting was concluded. Ample time to perpetrate murder at High Beeches.

18

Young Detective Constable Cox had been delighted to be given the assignment. Now he was not so sure.

He had tailed men on foot before, several times, but he had never tailed a car, let alone a woman in a car. And this was worrying territory for a novice. The A4136 which ran through the Forest of Dean to Monmouth was a road which wended its way round a series of inclines and descents. A picturesque drive, in other contexts, but a difficult road on which to tail a car.

If you stayed a respectable distance behind, as the book said you should do to escape notice, you risked losing your subject altogether, down one of the lanes which snaked abruptly away off this main route. If you stayed close, to avoid the possibility of such disaster, any quarry was likely to become suspicious of a car which remained in the rear-view mirror for mile after mile.

In the event, it was surprisingly easy. Alison Hargreaves had told her brothers that she thought the police might be watching her. But she did not give much attention now to the possibility of being followed. Perhaps that came from leading a law-abiding life for so long. More probably, she was too excited about the man she was going to meet to pay much attention to the traffic behind her. DC Cox tucked his grey Cavalier in behind a flashy red Mercedes, which, in spite of repeated efforts, found it impossible to pass Alison's ageing blue Fiesta on this winding road.

To Cox's relief, she did not turn on to any of the lanes, but drove right into Monmouth. Even when they crossed the fine old bridge over the Wye and stopped at the traffic lights on the fringe of the ancient town, he was sure that his pursuit had not been noted.

The narrow, busy streets of Monmouth presented different problems, but he did not have to disguise his presence for very long. Alison parked outside an old semi-detached house in a quiet cul-de-sac. She locked the car, but hardly looked behind her as she hurried in.

DC Cox parked a hundred yards away and waited. Once the woman had been inside for a couple of minutes, he used his car phone to report the address to DI Rushton. Then he settled down to wait.

Eve Brownrigg tucked the blanket carefully around her husband Charlie. The heating was quite warm enough for her, but you couldn't be too careful with invalids. Besides, fussing round the wheelchair gave her a moment to think.

'We're only checking up, you know. We're not trying to catch you out.' Hook's tone was persuasive, his sympathy for the reservations of Eve genuine. He had come here on his own, was deliberately avoiding the production of his notebook. In his own mind, he was sure this elderly couple had done no ill to Walter Fletcher, even if the facts gave them motive, means and opportunity.

Eve's old face was as sharp and intelligent as a mother bird's. Her husband was just delighted to have a visitor: his red face looked eagerly at his wife's to see how she would react to Hook's words. Charlie loved the thought of being able to help the police solve a murder mystery; he had not had such importance for years. It was like being in one of the books Eve brought him from the library.

Hook clasped his hands appreciatively round the china beaker. 'Good coffee, this. I like a mug: you get more and it stays hotter.' He grinned in male conspiracy at Charlie Brownrigg, who cackled a delighted agreement from his wheelchair.

'Now, you two.' Hook addressed himself to both of them, even though it was only Eve who would have been out and about on the day. 'We have been told that Bella, Dermot Fletcher's black Labrador, was around on the day before old Mr Fletcher was killed.'

'That he was,' said Eve promptly. 'And Dermot, too. I saw the two of them, up by Brenda Collins's house in the morning.'

'Dermot and the dog were together?'

She nodded, bridling a little that he should need to be told again. 'That's what I said. And I saw 'em again in the afternoon, didn't I? They were going back towards Endean, on the footpath.'

It was the first time anyone had mentioned seeing the boy with the dog. Everyone else had just presumed that he must be around. 'You're sure it was actually Dermot, Mrs Brownrigg? At a distance, you see –'

''Course I am. My eyes is as good as they were forty years ago, baint they, Charlie?' Her husband nodded vigorous agreement. 'Anyway, I spoke to him, didn't I? Near as I am to you now, I was, Sergeant Bert Hook!'

'When was this?'

She mused for a moment, enjoying her importance, conscious of Charlie's delight at her side. 'Monday afternoon. Day before old Mr Fletcher died. I presumed he'd been up to see old Walter, but he didn't say that, mind.'

'He was seen the next day, too. At least, Bella was.'

'If Bella was there, Dermot would be. Never saw the dog without him, did we, Charlie?' She drew the invalid in determinedly, and again Charlie Brownrigg nodded vigorous confirmation.

'Did they come up to High Beeches? You were working up there on that Tuesday morning, weren't you?'

'No. Never saw him nor the dog up there that day.' She paused, as a thought brought excitement rushing into her crafty, experienced old face. 'Unless he came after I'd left. That was at quarter past twelve.'

Alison Hargreaves stayed for two and a half hours at the house in Monmouth. Her departure was observed and

161

relayed as carefully by DC Cox as her arrival had been.

An hour after she had gone, Lambert's old Vauxhall eased into the drive of the semi-detached Victorian house. Superintendent and sergeant glanced up for a moment at the upper windows of the building, then went and rang the bell of the upper flat.

The man who opened the door to them recognized them as policemen as soon as he saw them. More than that: he knew within seconds that he had met one of them before. A few years back, in circumstances he chose not to recall.

He stood back and they moved unhurriedly past him into the long, high drawing room of his flat, with the new double-glazed window through which he had seen them arrive. The three men looked at each other for a moment, then sat down on the heavy three-piece suite. Not a word had passed between them until that point, though under-currents of understanding had flowed between them.

'Alex Moon,' said Lambert reflectively. 'Sergeant Alex Moon, of West Mercia CID.'

'Not any longer,' said the man in the armchair opposite him. 'Not for six years now. As you know better than most, Chief Inspector Lambert.'

'Superintendent now, Alex. And this is Sergeant Bert Hook.'

The man nodded briefly at Hook, noting that he was probably a good ten years older than he had been when he left the force, and still a sergeant. He did not know and would scarcely have believed that Hook had turned down the interviews for promotion to the rank of inspector. It was so rare in the force as to be highly suspect conduct.

Lambert said, 'Your security firm's doing good business, I hear, Alex.'

'Good enough. I've got a couple of decent contracts. And of course, the failures of the police to control crime mean that the demand for my services is constantly rising.' Moon smiled sourly at his joke.

'More flexible rule book, I imagine, too.' Lambert wasn't

going to be drawn into a row, but he could not resist reminding the man of why he had left the police.

'You did me a favour, you and your cronies, six years ago.'

'Not me, Alex. I just did my job, when I was brought in for the official enquiry. It was your actions that determined you should go.'

In the end, Sergeant Moon needn't even have gone, if he had chosen to brazen it out. The Crown Prosecution Service didn't want to take the case on, and the Chief Constable understandably didn't want the publicity. Coercing witnesses and beating prisoners wouldn't have made good headlines, for anyone.

'I was only trying to put away villains.' It was probably true: there had been no hint of payment from rival criminals, as there sometimes was in these cases. But Moon had been taking short cuts to get his convictions for years before he was pinned down. He had flouted the rule book he claimed to despise, and paid the penalty. In Lambert's view, he had got off lightly.

'We're not here to talk about old times, Alex.'

'No. I didn't think you were. Still, nice of you to ask how I'm getting on. I might be able to offer you a job, when it comes to supplementing your pension.' He eyed Lambert's greying temples with satisfaction.

'Alison Hargreaves, Alex. That's why we're here.'

He had known it from the start. The watchful look in his light-blue eyes gleamed brighter. 'Nice woman, Alison. I hope you're not going to –'

'How long have you been seeing her, Alex?'

Moon looked at Lambert. He had a score to settle with this man, but he could see no chance of doing that here. The policeman in him told him to play this carefully, be selfish. There was no way he could get himself into trouble here, unless he lied. Therefore, be honest, all the way, if possible. Sorry, Alison.

Moon switched to a carefully formal tone. 'I suppose

I've known Mrs Hargreaves for about six months now. Maybe a little longer.'

'I think you will have guessed by now why we are here. We are investigating the murder of Alison Hargreaves's father. On Tuesday, twenty-third October.'

'You're right. I did guess that.'

'How many people know about your relationship with Mrs Hargreaves?'

Moon shrugged. Keep cool. Remind them that you know the score. 'I couldn't say. She thinks no one does. You and I know that if you ask around enough, you usually find people who know. Or at least suspect.'

That was true enough, in general. But if any of the villagers of Endean knew about Alison's visits here, they had kept quiet about it when talking to the door-to-door team. That might be no more than the Foresters protecting their own. 'Does Jim Hargreaves know?'

Again that elaborate shrug, telling them how secure he felt, how little this mattered to his own safety. 'I've never met the man. Alison thinks he suspects nothing. She's probably right. That saying about the husband being the last to know is often correct, as I suppose you realize.' He allowed himself a tiny sneer of contempt on the last phrase.

'When the lady comes here, she takes pains to do so in secret, then?'

A condescending smile. 'As far as she knows how, yes. But your man followed her here today without her spotting him, didn't he?'

Lambert had the feeling that Alison would be well rid of this man. But he thrust aside a thought that was merely a distraction. 'Did Mrs Hargreaves come here on the afternoon of October twenty-third?'

Alex weighed the question carefully, though he knew well what his answer was to be. He decided he could safely string this out a little. 'She's told you that she was with her brother on that afternoon.'

'She has.' Lambert suspected that Moon knew that this

was her second version of that fatal afternoon, but he wasn't going to discuss that with this smug ex-copper.

'She wasn't, I'm afraid. She was here with me. In bed for most of the time, if you want to know.'

They didn't. Hook, carefully neutral, said, 'What time did she arrive and leave, Mr Moon?'

Alex looked at him, his broad face not troubling to disguise the contempt he felt for this time-server with his notebook. His luxuriant eyebrows lifted a little as he gave the impression of thinking about the figures he had already determined to give them. 'It would be about one o'clock when she got here, I suppose. She must have left at about three. She likes to be at home when her husband gets back from that school of his, I think.' His scorn for the cuckold he had never met stole for a moment across his flushed features.

He folded his arms. Lambert looked at his powerful forearms, at the huge hands which had beaten his prisoners into submission and brought him and Lambert briefly together six years ago. 'We'll need you to sign a statement in due course. You know the form.'

Alex Moon nodded, then hesitated, looking at the door into the hall, visualizing the bedroom beyond it with its tumbled sheets. He took a decision. 'You might as well know the whole story. When I'm helping the police with their enquiries, I go the whole hog.' He grinned patronizingly from one to the other, thinking how far behind he had left men like this.

'Well?' Lambert no longer troubled to disguise the dislike this man seemed determined to invite.

'Alison called at her father's house – High Beeches, is it? – on her way home from here. She wanted to talk to him, explain her reasons for asking him to move out of the place.' He paused; his arms were still resolutely folded, but he had dropped his eyes, for the first time since they had come into the room. 'She found the old man dead, of course. She left him there and went home.'

'And why didn't she report the death at the time?'

He shrugged once more, as if his broad shoulders were glad to be in action again. 'You'd have to ask her that. I think she just panicked and thought she'd be the first suspect. Well, she would have been, wouldn't she? PC Plod doesn't look too far, when he has a suspect who's had a row with the victim two days earlier.'

'And why did she lie to us about where she was that afternoon, when you could have confirmed that she was here?'

'Again, you will no doubt need to check that with her. But I know she didn't want her husband to find out about us. Not yet, anyway.' He smiled complacently.

Lambert could think of another reason. At that moment, it seemed an attractive one. A mistress and her lover, in search of funds to set themselves up together, were a common combination in murder.

19

Like all intricate bureaucracies, the police machine is subject to technical problems. Or cock-ups, as those within the system more usually call them.

And as with all bureaucracies, these mistakes are concealed as far as possible from the public. The one which complicated the investigation of the murder of Walter Fletcher was discovered just in time. As a result, few people outside the machine realized how near the case had come to degenerating into farce.

The complication stemmed, as such things usually do, from the complex and overlapping areas of police responsibility. When a man who is a leading murder suspect is held in custody for another offence altogether, that might be seen as an advantage to the CID, and indeed it would normally be so. But when investigations into two serious but unconnected crimes are being conducted in different geographical areas, by different police forces, there may be both complications and oversights. Cock-ups, in fact.

The man involved in this one was Dermot Fletcher.

When DI Rushton had journeyed north to Birmingham to question him, the young man had been in a sense a victim as well as a criminal, a victim of the poison he had been found purveying by the Drugs Squad. When Rushton questioned him, he had been able to provide no proper explanation of his whereabouts at the time of the death of his grandfather. He had admitted, indeed, that he could not remember where he was at the time.

Even if it was true, it was an unsatisfactory answer, and it was recorded in the swelling files of the investigation as such. But Dermot was remanded in custody when the charges relating to his supplying of drugs were committed to the Crown Court. The treatment for his addiction continued, with a measure of success.

Gradually, it became clear that he had been telling the truth about the murder of Walter Fletcher. At the time when Rushton had questioned him, Dermot Fletcher had genuinely not known where he was on Tuesday, twenty-third October.

It now emerged that other people did know where he had been on that fatal afternoon. People of impeccable reliability: the police themselves.

It was a rather embarrassed chief superintendent in Birmingham who rang John Lambert as he arrived that morning in his Oldford CID office. 'This lad Fletcher,' he said. 'Do you have him in the frame for a killing on the twenty-third of October?'

'In the frame, yes. Nothing more than that, at the moment. We've been investigating other leads, whilst you kept him safely in the hutch for us.'

'What time was this death?'

'Sometime between twelve-thirty and four on that afternoon.' Those were the limits that had been stated in the Coroner's Court, even if by now he had a more precise time in his own mind.

'Dermot Fletcher isn't your man, then. Unless you can have him as an accessory.'

Lambert paused, then said heavily, 'Where was he?'

'He was with us. Not here, but in a nick down the road. We brought him in at two in the morning on that day. In possession of a banned substance – no evidence of any dealing at that time. Stoned out of his mind. We kept Fletcher here until four that Tuesday afternoon, until we could get some sort of sense out of him. In the end, we sent him away with a caution.'

168

Lambert said, 'Thank you. It would have been helpful to know this earlier, but thank you.'

His irony brought the beginnings of apology and excuses, but he cut them short. As it happened, it wouldn't have helped the investigation a great deal to have had Dermot Fletcher ruled out earlier.

Coming now, the news merely sharpened the conclusion he had reached overnight.

Dermot Fletcher's father did not yet know that his son had been excluded by the police from suspicion of his grandfather's murder. But he was probably the only member of the family who had been certain from the beginning that his son was not involved in the old man's death.

The last summer cabbage and the last lettuces had gone to market some time ago now. Alan Fletcher had the rotavator out on this bright morning, turning the half-acre of vegetable patch over, so that the autumn rains and the winter frosts might do their work upon it.

The old machine worked fairly well, once he had managed to get it started. But there was a thin cloud of blue smoke around him, and the racket from the worn engine was deafening. Soon now, very soon, he would be able to purchase a new machine, more up to date, with automatic starting and a more powerful motor.

This might in fact be the last time he coaxed the old machine through a morning's work. Alan worked his way diligently across the rich red-brown soil of the plot; the faithful servant, so often repaired and so often cursed, should have a decent finale before it was laid to rest.

He was so preoccupied, and the rotavator was so noisy, that he neither saw nor heard the approach of the two large figures, who stood watching him turn the ground without any gesture towards interference. It was not until he had worked to the end of a line, and moved the machine through the two long shadows cast by the November sun, that he realized they were there.

169

Alan did not panic at the sight of the men who waited like angels of death at the edge of the soil. Instead, he held the bucking machine steady between his muscular forearms, turning up the power a little, until the roar seemed the only sound in miles of that quiet landscape and the damp soil flew higher, threatening to spatter the rich shine on the shoes of the men who had come out from the town to confront this sturdy country titan.

Alan Fletcher looked back down the lines of his furrows, appeared to find them satisfactory, and twisted back the throttle of the rotavator, so that its roar dropped first to an uneven rattle and then to a silence, which seemed the more profound after the cacophony which had preceded it.

The thin funnel of blue smoke died to a thread above the old green machine. They could smell the warm oil, feel the heat from the engine through the still cool of the autumn day. Alan said, 'Be you any nearer finding out who killed my old dad, then?'

He was a man who had scarcely moved outside the county, yet they had never heard his Gloucestershire accent so strong when they had seen him previously. It seemed as though in this final chapter, the Forest, which had held them at bay for so long in the attempt to protect its own, was asserting its identity even in defeat.

Lambert said, 'We're a lot nearer to an arrest, Alan. And your son has definitely been eliminated from our enquiries, now.'

Alan nodded, sinking his chin a little into his broad chest, lifting his broad fingers from the worn rubber handles of the rotavator, studying his hands for a moment as they tingled still from the vibrations of the work. 'I told you Dermot had nothing to do with it. I knew as 'ow you'd find I was right, in the end.'

'I believe you did know, Mr Fletcher. I believe, indeed, that you based most of your conduct upon that knowledge.'

It was both a warning and a challenge. Alan Fletcher

looked into their faces then for the first time. For an instant, his grey-blue pupils filled with speculation. Then he dropped them back to the machine and busied himself with easing it on to a dry patch of ground. 'I'll leave this here for a while,' he said. 'Won't do the old girl any harm to have a rest. We can talk inside, if you like.'

The big old farmhouse kitchen, with its Aga, its scrubbed deal table, its square of worn carpet, its shabby chairs and its round black and white clock, seemed by now a familiar place to them. The owner said, 'The kettle will be hot on the Aga. I'll make us a drink – it won't take a minute. Then you can tell me about what's been happening.'

As the outdoor man moved indoors, away from the ground he had worked for a quarter of a century and the Forest around it, his accent was blunted. He moved carefully to reach crockery, milk, sugar. There was something faintly ridiculous about his striving for the role of the conventional host.

Hook looked quickly at Lambert, then relaxed a little, allowing their man to make these simple domestic movements. Alan's voice had never faltered; now his hands were just as steady, as they busied themselves with beakers, coffee jar and biscuit tin. Bert Hook felt that they were watching the man pass some small, irrelevant test of nerve, which he had set for himself.

The dog, Bella, lifted herself a little stiffly from her position by the stove and came over to sit beside Hook when Fletcher produced the biscuits; strangers were always worth a little attention, in case they showed signs of weakness with food in their hands. She put her black muzzle on Hook's knee and gave him the full treatment from her soulful brown eyes, until Fletcher said sharply, 'Lie down, Bella!' and she was obliged to abandon her quest.

Lambert watched dog and master speculatively throughout the moment. Then he said, 'Bella is Dermot's dog. You insisted on that to us, when we asked about her.'

171

'You wouldn't be in any doubt of that, if you saw them together.' In that instant, his affection for the dog flooded over his face as he looked down at her. It was as if the love he felt for his son could be transferred in his absence to the beast the boy loved so much.

'I believe you, Alan. Not least because everyone else involved has told us the same thing.'

'He's a good boy, Dermot, you know. Well, a good man, I suppose I should say now. I know he's given you a bit of trouble, this last year or two. But that will soon be over, now.'

'A bit of trouble is putting it mildly. We know he isn't a murderer now, but he's still facing serious charges, you know.' Lambert, wanting to know how this man's mind worked, found himself drawn into talking about his son, though he knew that it was now irrelevant.

He might never have spoken, for Fletcher carried on as if he had not even heard him. 'He'll be all right, now, will Dermot. Now that . . .'

He ran out of words, then looked up suddenly at them, puzzlement turning for the first time to apprehension in his broad, revealing features. It was left to Lambert to complete his sentence for him. 'Now that you have secured the funds you wanted from your father, Alan.'

'Yes. That doesn't mean that I had anything to do with killing him.'

'The dog might have been bought for Dermot, all those years ago. That doesn't mean that she doesn't regard you as her master, when he isn't around. Bella follows you about all day, as you admitted.'

As if responding to the thought, the black Labrador moved across to Fletcher and placed her chin on his thigh, lifting her paw in a tiny gesture of supplication, turning her brown eyes full upon his face.

The Judas kiss, thought Alan bitterly. Then, in the same moment, he rejected the thought. There was no treachery, no calculation, in the dog's gesture. Nothing but the affection which he had used to cloak his actions at High

Beeches. He reached a hand to the dog's head, wishing that human devotion could be so uncomplicated.

Lambert looked at the pair, quiet and still as a Victorian painting. Yet the man was a murderer, the dog his innocent decoy. He said, 'You knew that when the dog was seen near your father's house, people would immediately assume that it was Dermot who was up there. So you took her with you – made sure, in fact, that she was seen.'

Fletcher suddenly looked very tired. He found that confession was going to be a relief, after all. He found that he was almost anxious to explain himself now. 'I knew that you wouldn't be able to pin the killing on Dermot, you see. You'd find out eventually that he was in police custody at the time. So there could be no real danger to him. I was the only one who knew that he couldn't have been there.'

'But just because you were the only one, Alan, you had to be chief suspect, once we knew that Dermot wasn't even in the area at the time.'

Alan Fletcher weighed this, seemed to approve it, and calmly went on with the explanation which would give him a life sentence. 'I'd argued with Dad on the phone, but he refused to listen to me. I explained that I needed the money for Dermot, so that we could work together, develop the business. But he said his grandson was a bad lot.'

Even now, the pain of the old man's rejection of his grandson was etched upon Alan Fletcher's face, making him oblivious to all else. Lambert said gently, 'He had taken money from your father, after all, when he was eighteen.' It sounded like an expiation of the old man's attitude to his grandson; in fact, he was only interested in prompting Alan to move forward with his grisly story.

'Dad reminded me of that, when I asked him to help. He even said he was going to cut Dermot out of his will altogether. Said if he helped him, it would just be throwing good money after bad. I couldn't take that. I had to act, before Dad got round to the will.'

'So you made your preparations with Bella, and went up to High Beeches to kill him.'

Alan Fletcher shrugged those massive shoulders for the final time. 'I don't know what I intended, when I went up there. But when the police rang through from Birmingham to say that Dermot was being held for possession of crack, I knew I must get money quickly, if he was to be put back on the right path.'

The logic of his love for his son overrode all other passions for him, even the love for his father he had evinced to them at an earlier interview. He did not even seem aware of the enormity of what he had done, in the face of his desperation about his son. He had a bizarre touch of pride as he said, 'So I thought up the plan with Bella, didn't I, girl?' He looked down at the dog as if he were talking of the indulging of a mere canine mischief.

'You went up to High Beeches with the intention of killing your father on that Tuesday afternoon.'

It was a bald statement from Lambert, challenging his man to deny it. But Fletcher had lost the taste for deceit, which had never come easily to him. A frown of genuine perplexity furrowed his wide forehead. 'I told you, I don't know what I intended. But I made the preparations, taking Bella up there. And when I saw Dad up the ladder, it seemed like fate. I thought of the things he'd said about Dermot, and I cut the tie on the ladder and flung Dad off it, all in one second.'

There was a moment of silence, as the horror of patricide flooded into the warm room. Then Lambert said quietly, moving them on from that awful picture, 'You're the practical one of the family, Alan. It struck us as odd when you said you weren't aware that your father fastened the ladder to the wall when he worked on that gable end.'

Fletcher nodded. 'I was the only one of the three of us who knew about that.' Then he said, seemingly so proud of the deceit that he could not hold it back from them, 'I told Alison last night to say she was with me on that Tuesday afternoon. She thought I was protecting her, but I was making her act as an alibi for me, really.'

For a moment, he was overcome by the thought of his own cleverness: neither Alison nor Chris would have thought old Alan capable of such subtlety, would they? It had been his clever plan which had brought them all what they wanted. And last night, when Alison had been grateful for his offer to protect her, he had been using her after all to cover his own traces.

The satisfaction in his cleverness was fleeting. In the next instant, the broad features darkened, as the enormity of his crime seemed for the first time to press upon him. He stared over the dog's head towards the Aga and the clock on the wall beyond it, the fingers of his right hand gently stroking the back of his left. But he saw nothing except the awful vision of a body, his father's body, plunging in a crazy arabesque to its death.

Then, suddenly and violently, Alan Fletcher's face was in his hands. The massive shoulders heaved. He sobbed, uncontrollably, tearlessly, awfully.

He went meekly enough to the car, accepting the handcuffs like a man in a dream. He sat beside Hook in the back as they drove through Endean. One or two curious faces stared in at him in the village, but they got no response from him.

In a few more minutes, they would be out of the Forest of Dean, where he had spent the whole of his life. The Forest which had seemed to the CID men in the car with him to throw a protective covering round this tragic family.

The sun was at its highest point of the day now, burnishing the crimsons and the ambers of the autumn leaves with gold. The car was at the rise of a hill when Alan Fletcher twisted his head for the only time. He looked back towards the nursery where he had striven so hard for so long.

'Dermot will have to develop our land, now,' he said proudly. 'At least the lad will have the money I never had, to make a go of it.'

Hook, sitting beside him, stared ahead and said nothing. A man would need his illusions, where Alan Fletcher was going.